WILD
GAME

WILDING PACK WOLVES 1

Alisa Woods

December 2015 Edition
Sworn Secrets Publishing

Cover Design by Steven Novak

ISBN-13: 978-1532729409
ISBN-10: 1532729405

Wild Game (Wilding Pack Wolves 1)
Her pack is being hunted.
He's a bodyguard with a secret.
The Wolf Hunter is targeting them both.
GAME ON.

Owen Harding hasn't shifted since he was in Agent Smith's experimental cages—the only thing this ex-Army Texas boy is afraid of is what kind of beast he's become. But with a hate group issuing more threats against the Wilding pack than you can shake a stick at, Owen's doing what he can as a personal bodyguard. If only the Wilding girl he's tasked with keeping alive wasn't so damn sexy… and completely off limits.

Nova Wilding's father was assassinated, leaving her a gaming company to run, a new game to release, and a pack full of wolves who want her for a mate… including a beta who's determined to have Nova *and* her company. Choosing someone outside the pack will tear it apart, but Nova can't stop watching the hot shifter who's keeping watch over her.

When Nova barely escapes an attempt on her life, she finds herself in Owen's arms… but her sexy new bodyguard is absolutely the wrong man at the wrong time. While Nova fights to keep her father's business afloat, and Owen fights to keep her alive, the *Wolf Hunter* is playing a dangerous new game that might destroy them both.

CHAPTER 1

Owen Harding was surrounded by wounded warriors.

He wasn't one of them—at least, not that anyone could tell from the outside. They were lying in their VA Hospital beds, the war having snatched away their arms and legs and flash-burned faces like it was collecting parts for a grisly soldier bingo. Owen had done three tours with the Army in Afghanistan, but the sight of his fellow warriors in various states of damage still made him want to kick the war's ass. He didn't know these soldiers, but he knew the type—back when he was Private First Class Owen Harding, he had been just like them, wanting to give everything he had to protect the country he loved.

Then his country betrayed him.

No, that wasn't fair. He knew the country was filled with good people... but it had its share of bad. And it wasn't the entire country, anyhow, or even the whole military. It was one, single jackass Colonel with his grand ideas and lack of morals. He was the one who planted the IED that blew up Owen's life and sent him into a hellhole of a medical prison. That Colonel also authorized the experiments that Agent Smith performed on Owen and countless other shifters. It didn't mollify Owen much that Smith and the Colonel were both either dead or up on charges. There was nothing more to be done about it, but that didn't mean Owen wouldn't be paying for it like a bad night in Vegas... in other words, for the rest of his life. Some soldiers carried their injuries on the outside; for others, the war stole a part of their minds. For him, the military took something even worse—the thing that made a man what he was.

Owen simply didn't know anymore.

He had started out the war as a man and a wolf—a

shifter putting his skills in the service of his country—
and then Agent Smith's experiments turned him into
some kind of monster. The kicker was, he didn't even
know what kind. Nor did he feel like rushing in and
finding out. He didn't want to say he was afraid to
know… but that was exactly how it was.

"How's it going in there?" The voice came through
the earbud stuck in his ear. That was Murphy, part of
Riverwise Private Security, Owen's new employer. Owen
was semi-permanently assigned to bodyguard Nova
Wilding, current CEO and lead game developer of
Wylderide Gaming, but Murphy and Simpson were just
on loan for today's excursion. "Anytime you're ready to
swap places, Owen, just let me know. I want a shot at
that new beta version of *Domination*."

"Domination?" Owen replied through the mic clipped
to his shirt collar. "Is that a computer game or something
ya'll do with Simpson on the weekends?" *Domination:
AfterPulse* was Wylderide's latest futuristic combat game.
It was still in beta, but the wounded warriors were playing
an exclusive demo on borrowed laptops, courtesy of
Nova. This was a charity event, some kind of joint league
play set up just for the soldiers at the VA. Owen didn't
play, but he knew a lot of gamers, both in the service and

back home in Texas.

"You're such an asshole," Murphy's voice squeaked in his ear. "You *know* I'm dying to get my hands on that thing. Not to mention the lead developer herself."

Owen scowled, even though Murphy couldn't see him from where he was stationed outside the hospital. "I didn't realize Riverwise's professional standards now include groping clients." He put some warning into his voice. They were here to protect Nova from the hate group that had murdered her father and were targeting the entire Wilding pack… not to disrespect and ogle her, even on chatter. "Do I need to rotate you out and bring in a new volunteer?"

"No, sir." Murphy's voice was chastened. "Just noting the obvious, sir."

"And that would be?"

"That Nova Wilding is brightening the day of many soldiers today, sir."

"Copy that." Owen swept the room with his gaze until he found Nova again. She'd been his personal responsibility for nearly a month, ever since her father was murdered, and she pretty much never left his sight. Fortunately, the vast majority of Nova's waking hours were spent at Wylderide, where her father had been CEO before her—and the office was relatively secure on the twenty-fourth floor of a high-rise in downtown Seattle. This charity event was a lot more vulnerable.

But Murphy was right—Nova Wilding was easy on the eyes.

He watched her flit from one warrior to the next, her long, jet-black hair bound up to keep it off the keyboards. She had a brilliant blue streak running the length of it, and a strand had worked loose. It kept falling across her face, and she kept tucking it behind her ear—looked like a losing battle to him. Her bio put her at twenty-two, not much younger than Owen's twenty-six, but the gulf was more than just years. His time on the planet couldn't be any more different than hers. Plus she was about as big as a minute—petite body, delicate little fingers, yet with the wiry strength of a gymnast when she was running wires through the ceiling of the office or toting equipment into the event. For the tournament, she was decked out in combat gear—not the standard black body armor you might see in the service, but some kind of custom job, almost a costume tailored to her tiny form and crafted to resemble the gear from the game.

There was no question she was smokin' hot. The eyes of every veteran followed her as she went from bed to bed, checking their equipment and showing off the new gameplay features. Owen recognized the longing in their eyes—he had that same, gut-twisting ache that came from too much combat and too few women in his life.

In fact, Nova was about the only one—and he'd seen a lot of her in action over the last month. She was all about the company's flagship game most of the time, but given it was basically military ops, she had a lot of respect for service personnel and the sacrifices they made. This event was her idea, in spite of being in mourning for her father... or perhaps because of it. She'd pulled all the pieces together—high-quality gaming gear donated by the company, permission to operate at the VA, even created a special server for them—and she'd been here since early this morning, setting up the network and testing it out.

Right now she was going back and forth between two vets who were whooping and hollering like idiots, flailing around with their good arms and nearly dumping their laptops. One of them was missing an arm, the other had one in a sling. Owen couldn't tell if their mile-wide grins were from an excess of painkillers or the fact that Nova was bending over their laptops, syncing their games or whatever she was doing.

The two grunts exchanged smirk-filled looks, then burst out in laughter.

Nova glanced between them with an uncertain look.

Owen was manning his position by the door, but even from a dozen yards away, he could see the crinkled expression on her pretty face and the tight set of her lips. She backed away from them and scanned the room, looking for something. When her gaze fell on him, she hesitated, then dropped her gaze.

Something was up.

He knew all her body signals at this point, even if their conversations had never gone much past *Good Morning* and *God, I need coffee.*

He started toward her. "Checking in with NovaCaine," he said into his mic. "Going mic silent for a moment."

She was still staring at a spot on the floor when he arrived. "Everything all right, ma'am?"

She looked up and seemed a little surprised to see him there. She probably didn't notice him anywhere near as much as he noticed her. But then that was his job. Hers was to keep her father's gaming business afloat.

She shook her head—they weren't far from the two gamer vets—and turned to walk back toward the door he had just come from. An orderly glided through just as they arrived, and Owen took a moment to check out his ID. It was one of the younger male nurses, and Owen recognized him from before, so he turned his attention back to Nova.

"Is there something I can help you with, ma'am?" he asked again.

She grabbed hold of the loose string of blue hair, twisted it, then cast a look back at the soldiers. She had a habit of doing that—playing with her hair when she was thinking about something.

He waited.

She turned back to him. "Do you think they'd be more comfortable if I weren't around?" Her eyes were dark as midnight and twice as serious.

He frowned. "No, ma'am, I don't. Not quite sure I take your meaning, though."

She released her hair. "I was hoping the game might bring back some of that sense of camaraderie for them. But they seem to, I don't know, act a little strange when I'm around? I'm thinking maybe, if I wasn't distracting them, they might enjoy the game more."

She must not have felt the heat of a million stares on her illegally cute bottom.

He held back his smirk as much as possible. "No, ma'am. These grunts have each other's ugly mugs to look at all day long, every day. You're doing a good thing here, breaking up the monotony. They just don't know quite what to do with, well, the improved scenery you've brought to their day."

She gave him a puzzled look. "Improved scenery? The game is set in a futuristic post-apocalyptic combat zone, as realistic as we could—"

Owen couldn't help it—his laugh burst out of him. It cut her off quickly, and her pale cheeks pinked up, like little roses under those charcoal-lined eyes.

"You are the scenery, Ms. Wilding. No disrespect, ma'am, but they haven't seen anything as good-looking as you in a long time. Certainly not something at their bedsides." He struggled mightily to keep the grin off his face, but it would have been easier to catch a firefly with his teeth.

Her face opened with surprise then a frown took over. She shook her disapproval at the floor. Owen wasn't sure what that was about.

She peered back up at him. "Nova," she said with a tight-lipped expression.

"How's that?" He must have missed something.

She scowled. "You've been watching over me for a month, Owen Harding. I think it's time you called me by my first name."

So she *had* noticed. He let that smile come out to play a little. "Yes, ma'am."

She rolled her eyes, then turned on her black-booted heel to stride back to the soldiers in their beds. This time, she had a wide, flirtatious smile for them, and he'd be damned if they didn't perk up twice as much as before. He suspected their playing skills were about to degrade substantially.

Nova Wilding wasn't just hot, and obviously kind, she was also smart enough to run the gaming company her father had dropped in her lap when he died. Apparently, charming soldiers who had been wounded in the course of their duty was also in her skillset.

A tightness crept into his chest. She was just the kind of woman he could really go for... if he wasn't such a fucking mess.

Damaged goods. That was about all he was now. During the year he'd been imprisoned, the suppressor kept him from shifting most of the time... except for those few times when Agent Smith tried to force it by injecting him with some serum or another. Owen always believed the shift was simple magic, but maybe it was biochemistry after all.

He hadn't gone to college, but he was a straight-A student before he got the hell out of that small, dirt-scrambling Texas town he grew up in. He knew a few things, and he learned a whole lot more in the Army. Agent Smith had been doing genetic experiments—on him, on hapless civilians, on a whole bunch of people—trying to create some kind of super shifter soldier. And Owen had seen some grisly, horrible things come out of it. People who weren't people—or wolves—but some kind of half mutant thing in between. Whatever that alternate form was supposed to be, a lot of them couldn't shift back because the result was such a freakish thing it kicked the bucket right away. It was a fucking Island of Dr. Moreau in that prison. Smith was dead now, but his legacy lived on… inside Owen's body.

Even after he was free, Owen had been afraid to shift. He couldn't summon his wolf anymore, and he was afraid to call it, anyway—who knew what kind of beast would show up? Figuring out that mystery might just be the last two seconds of his life.

But no shifting meant finding a mate got shoved right off the table of possibilities. Of course, he could mess around with human women, but Owen didn't like the idea of exposing anyone to the thing he had inside him. Not when he didn't know what it was himself.

Which meant work had absorbed all his attention.

Work... and watching Nova Wilding's very attractive, little rear end. It wasn't just her screaming hot body—it was getting to see all the sides of her with near 24/7 exposure. The days she straggled in after coding all night. The smiles she dragged out even when her eyes were hollowed after the funeral. And now the full-press flirtation show she was putting on for the soldiers playing her game.

Those boys were sure to be dreaming about her tonight.

But this desire of hers to give them a little relief... she was driving straight into his heart with that. Which started to be dangerous territory for him. These soldiers might recover, or even get fitted up with some fancy cybernetic limbs, but there was no physical therapy that could erase Owen's genetic damage, whatever it was.

That was a ticking time bomb waiting inside him.

One of Wylderide's employees, Brad Hoffman, came up to Nova and whispered something in her ear. Owen didn't like the way his hand settled at the small of her back, a little possessive gesture from the resident company alpha asshole. It had taken Owen approximately five seconds to peg Brad as the Wilding pack member most eager to claim Nova as his mate. Although Brad and Nova seemed to fight as often as they had a civil thing to say to one another.

It wasn't long before they started wrapping up. Nova visited each and every soldier with a hug before collecting up their laptop. A lot of grateful faces were left in her wake.

While Brad and two others started breaking down the gear, Nova strode up to him. "These guys will load up the van. I'm ready to go." She looked tired.

"Yes, ma'am," he said, automatically. She gave him a scowl that yanked a smirk right out of him. "I mean, yes, Mistress NovaCaine."

She mouthed the words *Oh my God,* then strode past him, but he thought he caught a glimpse of a smile on her.

Owen spoke into his mic. "NovaCaine on the move. Clear the car." He kept pace with her pretty easily—she barely came up to his shoulder, and those pretty little legs didn't get up much in the way of speed.

"NovaCaine?" she asked, giving him the side-eye.

"Have you been playing without me realizing it?"

NovaCaine was her gamer handle—he'd just taken to using it as her codename for their internal communications. He'd slipped up, using it in front of her.

"No, ma'am, er… Nova." It didn't sit right, calling her by her first name when he was supposed to be security. "Not a gamer, sad to say."

She gave him a skeptical look. "You should give it a try. I could teach you, but you might need a little weapons practice first." She smirked.

He might've spent a year languishing in a cage, but it wasn't like he'd forgotten how to shoot a gun. "I expect I won't get the same recoil from firing a keyboard." He returned her smirk. "But I won't pass up personal lessons if that's what you're offering." Did he really just say that? What was he thinking?

She ran her gaze over him in a way that wasn't at all unpleasant. "I don't have much time for casual play anymore… but I might make an exception for the man who's in charge of making sure I live through the day."

"Sounds like a fair trade." But his heart was thumping a little too hard for just walking.

They had reached the outside of the VA hospital, and the bright Seattle sunshine lit up the street. The VA was an entire campus of medical buildings, tree-lined lanes, and supporting businesses. The black sedan Owen had borrowed from Riverwise stood waiting for them, along with the River pack member who had volunteered to be Nova's driver. Her father had been killed by a car bomb, so they swept for those every time. The sedan's windows were rolled down, and Murphy and Simpson were just finishing up their sweep under the vehicle, looking for incendiary devices.

"All clear," Murphy said, pulling the long-handled electronics detector out from under the car. Owen did his habitual sweep of the street, but everything looked normal—several cars parked along the winding, tree-dappled lane, some light traffic winding around the VA complex.

He held open the door for Nova, and she stepped into the backseat. Owen barely got the door closed behind him when something small and metallic flew through the back seat window. Time slowed. He vaguely noticed a car driving past. His heart thudded once in his chest, then sunk to his stomach. The grenade tumbled to the floor and nestled right between Nova's boot-clad feet.

"Grenade!" He screamed and dove for it, knocking Nova into the cushion seat with one hand while the other

grabbed at the grenade. Somehow he grasped it by his fingertips and flung it out the window. Then he slammed Nova down on the car seat and covered her body with his. A deafening blast heaved the car into the air and tumbled them.

Nova screamed. He kept hold of her as the car flipped, pulling her tight against him and bracing out with his other arm. The car rolled, then dropped to a rest. She landed hard on his chest, and his back slammed against the roof, which was now the floor. Shouts sounded outside the car. Owen's ears rang from the blast, and a sharp pain seared his chest... but it was only Nova's claws. They had come out and dug into him, holding on for dear life.

He kept his arms locked around her, but he dipped his face down. "You all right?"

She gasped in air, then let out a squeak when she saw her claws ripping through the starched white fabric of his shirt. "Oh God, I'm sorry!" Her hands shifted back to human, and she tried to squirm away from him, but he just held her tight.

"*Nova Wilding,* tell me if you are injured," he demanded in his best command voice.

She stopped her squirming and looked up into his

face. Her eyes were wide and panicked. "No, I... I don't think so."

"Then I'm getting you out of here." He needed her calm so he could remove her from the scene as quickly as possible.

She nodded shakily. He lifted her off his chest, and they managed to crawl out the window. Murphy helped her, and Owen followed quickly.

"What the fuck was that?" Murphy was yelling at someone around the side of the car, but Owen didn't give a shit about explanations at this point. He had to get her away from here.

He grabbed onto Murphy's arm to get his attention. "You secure the scene and call the police. I'm getting her out of here."

Owen didn't wait for a response, he just swept his arm around Nova's waist and practically lifted her off the ground as he hurried her down the sidewalk. He hunched his body around hers to protect her from any possible sniper shots or backup grenade-wielding assailants that might be positioned in case the first attempt went wrong. Hell, for all he knew, the first attempt was just a set up for the real attempt to follow. She was far from out of danger.

He quickly glanced back at the wreckage of the car. The grenade had detonated out in the street, wiping out two trees and throwing shrapnel into a car across the street… but the worst of it was the driver. He lay motionless on the pavement, in pieces. The car itself had flipped onto its roof on the sidewalk, taking out another tree and smashing out the windshield.

But none of that was his concern. His only thought was getting Nova to safety.

He'd already outlined a safe location in the event of something like this, so without thinking, his legs carried them there. Down two streets, past a medical building, up a small winding tree-lined path. The VA complex was vast… they just needed a secure spot to retreat to until the threat was cleared. A loading dock loomed above them. Owen ushered her up the stairs and into the back side of the medical supply shop he had picked out as a safe retreat.

There was no one in the warehouse, but Owen still pulled her all the way to the back between stacks of giant cardboard boxes and metal supply shelves.

He spoke into the mic. "I've got NovaCaine sequestered. Let me know when ya'll secure the building."

Now that he had released her, Nova backed up against one of the large stacks of cardboard boxes and stared at him with wide eyes. She was shaking so hard, her hair was fluttering around her face. His heart clenched, and he moved toward her on instinct. He took her by the shoulders and scanned her body. Dirt scuffed her costume body armor, but that was it, as far as he could see.

"Are you sure you're all right?" he asked again.

"Y…yes." But the word was even more jittery than she was.

He pulled her into a hug. His hold was tight, pressing her to his chest, one hand secure around her back, the other holding her head against him. It was how he would hold a wild animal when it was frightened—locked down tight, nowhere to run, no sense in struggling. It calmed them… and it seemed to work on Nova as well. She made a little whimper sound and sunk into his chest, her hands bunching up the lapels of his jacket and burying her face.

"Hey, now, darlin', it's over," he said as softly as he could. "You're fine now. No need to worry. We will stay put, right here, until everything's clear." He could feel the tremors in her body. It gave him the most peculiar feeling—a pure sort of satisfaction that she was willing to let him hold her mixed with a heady kind of rush that made him want more full-body clinging in his future.

Her head shook against him, like she wasn't buying whatever he was sellin'.

"I promise, you're safe," he repeated. "This spot is as secure as it gets, given no one knows where we are. And I'm not fixin' to leave until I know it's safe out there again." The rumble of his words seemed to stop the shaking. Her hair had worked loose and formed a sort of black halo around her head. His fingers worked into it, massaging and soothing her. He hoped.

"Why?" she asked in a breathless whisper against his chest. "Why do they keep doing this?"

Why were people trying to kill this amazing, beautiful woman? He didn't have a good answer for that. Sure, the experiments that had been done on shifters like him had been exposed, and most decent folks were appalled, but some weren't. And when a brave lady shifter stepped forward to run as the first openly shifter member of the House of Representatives… well, that just tipped the haters right over the edge. They doxed the River and Wilding packs—posted their personal information on a video on YouTube—and ever since, the threat of violence had hung over shifters everywhere. An asshole hate group had already taken credit for blowing up her father in a car bomb—what better way to terrorize the rest of the shifter world than to follow that up with a grisly death for his daughter?

"They're evil bastards," Owen said. It was the only explanation he had for some things in this world.

Her head started shaking again. Definitely a *no*. "I should never have come. I risked everyone's life with this—"

He leaned back, not letting her go, but enough that he could peer down into her face. "Hang on now, you did a good thing here. This wasn't nothing you did wrong. These haters are pure evil on the earth—*they* are responsible for this. If anything, this is my fault for not keeping a closer watch. That will not happen again." It was slicing pain through him that somehow he hadn't seen this coming... although a drive-by grenade toss wasn't exactly something you could plan for. He hoped like hell someone had gotten a better look at the vehicle than he did—he couldn't even identify the color to save his life.

Nova peered up at him with those big, dark eyes. "You're going to protect me." She said it like a statement.

"Yes, ma'am." He wasn't certain of much else except that.

The charcoal lining around her eyes had started to smudge, like she had fought back tears but lost the battle. Her lips parted, and her chest heaved against his. Her nearness like this… this was a dangerous thing. He should let her go. But no way would he release her until she was ready. She let go of her hard grip on his jacket and flattened her hands against his chest.

Then she took a breath and repeated, "You're going to protect me." But it was softer this time.

"Always. I promise, Nova." His voice had grown soft because somehow… something had changed.

Suddenly, she slid her hands up his chest and grabbed the back of his head, pulling him down. She lifted up on her toes, and it was clear she aimed to kiss him. It took less than half a second of her lips on his before he was definitely giving as much as he was getting.

His arms unlocked so his hands could press into her back and bring her closer. Her mouth opened to his, and he didn't wait for any more invitation. He plunged in deep, tasting her, devouring what she eagerly offered. It was insane and intense… before he could get his head straight, he had her backed up against the cardboard boxes, pinning her petite armor-clad body with his. His hands plunged into her hair and angled her head to demand even more. He lost sense of everything—the time, the place, knowing this was neither of those. He just reveled in her tongue twisting with his, her teeth nipping at him, the small whimpering sound in her throat that was driving him mad. His body literally ached for more, his mouth watering to taste her everywhere. He was losing his mind in this kiss—

"Owen? Owen, report! Are you all right?" The earbud squawked in his ear, and he jerked back, suddenly breaking the kiss.

His breath was heaving, and her lips were swollen. It took him a full two seconds to come back to his senses and realize how completely messed up this was.

He slowly reached for the mic clipped to his collar. *Shit.* Had they heard all of that? "Uh... yes. Everything's fine."

"Strange sounds coming over your mic." It was Murphy. "Thought maybe you were in trouble."

Owen held Nova's wide-eyed gaze. "No, we're good. Probably a mic malfunction from the blast. Turning it off for now—audio still active. Notify me when ya'll get the place clear."

"Copy that."

Nova's gaze dropped, and she straightened her black body armor unnecessarily, smoothing her kiss-mussed hair back in place. That pink tinge had returned to her cheeks.

She'd never looked so beautiful as she did now, right after he had thoroughly kissed her. A tight feeling in his chest told him to stop, move back, apologize... all the things he had no interest in doing. Instead, he moved into her again, stopping just short of touching her. Or kissing her. Although he desperately wanted to do both.

"Next time you want to kiss me," he said, still breathing hard, "remind me to turn off my mic."

She shook her head in small rapid movements, looking everywhere but at him. "I can't kiss you."

He leaned closer. "Is that right? Because I'd say you definitely know how." Why was she pulling back? Just because he was a lowly Army grunt? Or her bodyguard? Never mind that Owen had trampled over every line of professionalism there was... somehow, he didn't think that was it. Hell, he had no idea why she'd kissed him in the first place, much less decided not to do it again.

"I just... can't do this." She put her hands on his chest again and pushed him away.

He backed up all the way to the far shelving, giving her a dozen feet of room. He'd heard about the Wilding females, and how they were beyond hot in the sack... but he didn't know what to do with this kind of hot and cold. Actually, he didn't know what to do with any of it.

She pointed a finger at him, but it was shaking. "This never happened. You tell no one."

"Yes, ma'am." But it stoked an angry fire in him. Clearly, he wasn't quite good enough for her. Not that she was wrong about that, but it still burnt his shorts.

She folded her arms and retreated against the cardboard boxes again. Some of Owen's anger dissipated in a wave of concern. What the fuck was he doing? Taking advantage of her distraught emotional state after she'd almost been blown up? Then feeling rejected because she didn't want to carry on more in the back of the medical supply warehouse?

He really wasn't that kind of asshole.

"Are you sure you're okay?" He kept his voice soft.

She nodded. But it was still shaky. "I just want to go home."

Fortunately, Murphy chose that moment to speak up again. "All clear. Owen, you can bring her in. Or we'll come your way. We've got alternate transport."

Owen clicked his microphone back on. "Copy that." To Nova's perked up interest, he said, "Let's get you home, then."

He escorted her all the way back to the office, then home to her apartment, careful to keep his distance, just like before, and to betray nothing on his face or in his demeanor that would hint to anyone watching that anything untoward had happened in that medical supply warehouse.

But he'd be damned if he wouldn't be replaying that kiss in his bed tonight.

Chapter 2

She could have died.

Nova had gone back to the office, then her apartment, then spent most of the night not sleeping. She had gotten up the next morning, had her breakfast, met Owen at the door of her apartment, took a silent ride to Wylderide without speaking to him, claimed the entire pot of coffee from the break room along with her mug, and retreated to her office.

Half the morning had passed, and through all of it,

she'd had lots of thoughts. Thoughts about the new beta edition they were about to launch. Thoughts about how she was going to keep the pack together long enough to get it released. And, sneaking in every once in a while when she least expected it, thoughts about how she could've *died* yesterday... and none of it would've made a damn bit of difference.

Which made her think about that kiss.

The one that took her by surprise and set her body and soul on fire.

She hadn't said a thing to Owen. *Shit,* she couldn't even look him in the eye. She'd spent a month watching him watch her, dreaming about how hot he was with those *Yes, Ma'ams* and that sultry Texas accent and his military politeness... then she damn near attacked him in that warehouse. Then, just as fast, she pushed him away.

He was the wrong man. Thoroughly wrong. Wrong in every way.

And that had freaked her out so badly she'd done the only thing she could—the only thing she ever did with men—she shoved him away.

This... to a man who had just saved her life.

It filled her with a hot-cheeked shame that was all mixed up with the kind of heat that pooled between her legs. She was so messed up.

She could've died yesterday.

No, check that. She *would* have died if it hadn't been for Owen Harding and his quick-witted reaction of just picking up the goddamn grenade and throwing it out of the car. *Jesus,* who did that? Who had the presence of mind to actually pull something like that off? If she thought he was hot before, with those broad shoulders and sexy shifter muscles, seeing him in action, literally saving her life, hauling her away to safety, reassuring her with his freakishly sexy body wrapped around her... well, it had been too much for her. She'd folded into him with the willpower of a crack addict. But his overwhelming hotness was a pretty shitty excuse for treating him the way she did afterward. She knew that. But if she kissed him again, she knew herself—one thing would have led to another, and she'd have been riding that cowboy faster than he could say *Thank you, ma'am.*

The only right thing she did in that warehouse was tell him the truth—that she *couldn't* kiss him. The wolves in her father's pack had been angling to claim her as a mate for *years.* Since her father's death, the jostling had only gotten more intense. The pack had no alpha now, and they needed one—Wylderide needed one—and she knew eventually she would have to take one of them as a mate. Or pick someone else who could bring the pack together. Right at the funeral, she had put them all on notice—she wouldn't be taking a mate until she had properly mourned the passing of her father and given a solid think-through to the future of the company. That held them off, but only barely. And Owen Harding, her sexy bodyguard, wasn't even close to the right pick. He was hot and brave and sexy as sin... but taking him for a mate would tear the pack apart. And destroy her father's company. She couldn't afford to be stupid like that... she had a business to run.

Nova gazed out the window of her office at the high gloss of sun on Seattle's downtown. Almost dying tended to put things in a different perspective. Living in the moment—like that moment when Owen pressed her up against those boxes and kissed the hell out of her—made sense when you'd just snatched life back from the gaping maw of death.

But the crazed anti-shifter hate group that killed her father would be very happy if she lived recklessly for today and let her father's company come crashing down as a result. No matter what, she couldn't let that happen. They were terrorists, and she'd be damned if she would let them win, not on her watch. She wasn't a soldier—not like those brave men she spent the day with, hopefully giving them a little respite from the price they'd paid to defend their country—but she knew that giving in to this hate group and what they wanted was flat wrong.

What *she,* Nova Wilding, wanted didn't matter. *That* did.

Nova tore herself away from the window and sunk down into the oversized leather chair at her desk. She'd locked up her father's office right after the funeral—his chair was the only thing she had pulled out before sealing it off. She couldn't even begin to think about going through his things. As far as she was concerned, they could leave everything as a shrine to the way he had built this company from scratch. The darkened, shade-pulled windows of his office reminded everyone, including her, why they were pressing on with the release of *Domination* on schedule. The chair she was sitting in reminded her even more, every day, that he was still there in spirit with her, holding her up, encouraging her. She knew he would have released this beta on time if there was any way possible to do it. She was just as sure that he planned for her to pick one of the fine wolves he had collected into his pack over the years as a mate so she could take over his company someday.

It just wasn't supposed to be *this* day. Or any day soon.

The screen in front of her blurred with sales projections, social media management, advertising budgets, a shitload of other stuff... why couldn't she just stick to coding? Or game development? That she understood. This, the business part... she grew up with it, but the details were all still new to her.

She dropped her head into her hands. How was she ever going to pull this off? It had been a month since her father was murdered, the deadline for the release was looming, and she had never felt more lost.

That's what kissing Owen really was about— forgetting all of it for a moment. Now she was back to reality, and somehow, she had to make reality work. She was trying to sort through and figure out the spreadsheets on her screen when a tap came at the door.

It opened, and Brad strode in, not waiting for permission. Owen was stationed out outside her door, like normal, and the icy glower he had for Brad surprised her a little. Normally, Owen's face was army-stoic, except for that fire in his eyes when she had pushed him away...

Brad closed the door behind him, cutting off her view

of Owen's dark look.

"Hey, hot stuff." Brad moved swiftly around her desk and took her by the hand, pulling her out of her chair. He had her in his arms before she thought to push back. He peered at her and frowned. "Are you okay? You looked pretty shook up for that two and half seconds you spent in the office yesterday after the attack. I called your cell a bunch of times, but you never picked up."

Nova just shook her head and stepped back, well out of reach. "Just needed some time to… sort things out."

He looked pained. *"God,* Nova… I told you that was a bad idea going to the VA."

She squeezed her eyes shut—that was the last thing she needed to hear right now. She opened her eyes to glare at him. "You think I don't feel bad about what happened? My driver *died,* Brad. *I* could've died." She opened her mouth to say more, but she couldn't force the words out to describe all the jumbled feelings inside her.

He came closer, his large hands reaching for her shoulders. "I know," he said softly. "It's been killing me, thinking about it all night."

She wanted to pull away, but his dark magnetism drew her in. He held her tight, and it was times like these that she wondered why she worked so hard at pushing him away. Of all the wolves in her father's pack, he was the natural pick. He was good-looking, but that wasn't it. He had a strength about him that enveloped her. He was such an alpha's alpha—sometimes she felt lost in his presence. And she hated that feeling. It smothered her, and if she was his mate... the magic would make that feeling overwhelming. And permanent.

"You don't need to worry about me," she said, even though it felt reassuring that he did.

"All I do is worry about you." He moved his hand up from her shoulder to run a finger along her cheek. "You know how I feel about you."

He'd made no secret that he wanted her for a mate and would fight anyone in the pack for her. Which was completely barbaric and ridiculous... and also pretty damn hot.

"I told you, I'm not ready for that." She leaned away from him, but he didn't let her go.

"It's been a month, Nova." His strong hands eased her close again, and he slipped his hand into her hair, around the back of her head. "I know you're still mourning... but I also know you need what I have to offer." Then he leaned in, and before she could protest, his lips were on hers, firm and demanding. He had kissed her before, during times of weakness when his attention broke her down, and her body always betrayed her, responding to his... as if her wolf couldn't resist his overwhelming alphaness. His tongue swept across her lips, then pressed inside, demanding that she let him into all the dark corners of herself. Her wolf had been begging her to take Brad to bed forever—to let him run those rough, strong hands all over her naked body—but now she was just whimpering off to the side, waiting it out, suddenly cold to the charms that normally had her panting.

Brad must have felt it because he pulled back and frowned. "I know you're scared, baby. Anyone would be. I'll get Riverwise to send us more security. I'm sure they'll want to after yesterday, anyway. And I don't want you leaving the office for any reason other than to go straight home."

She pulled away from him, untangling completely from his arms. "You don't give me orders, Brad Hoffman." She turned her back on him and stalked to the window, clenching her fists at her side.

She felt him come up behind her. "Those aren't orders, Nova. They're just common sense. You've got to protect yourself—"

"I am protecting myself!" She whirled back to him. "I can't stop living my life just because there's someone out there who wants to end it."

"It won't be this way forever," Brad said, a truly pained look on his face. "Don't fight me on this, Nova, I'm just trying to look out for you. Like your father would have."

"My father is dead because of these people." The fire was rising in her voice. "I'm not giving them what they want by cowering and hiding."

Brad shook his head and gazed out at the city, biting his lip like he was trying to summon the tremendous patience he needed to deal with her.

She was very tempted to tell him to fuck off and get out of her office. "Did you just come here to see if I was still alive? Or did you have some actual business?"

He looked wounded, but she didn't care—he should know better than to order her around. That was the fastest way to piss her off. The only time she had ever butted heads with her father was when he tried to tell her where she could go and what she could do. Which was part of why he always made it clear that choosing a mate was *her* decision, not his.

Brad took a deep breath. "Actually, I came in to talk about the new offer from the console guys."

A fresh fire rose up inside her. "No. Way."

"You haven't even heard the offer, Nova." He gave her a patronizing look.

"I don't need to, *Brad*. You know how I feel about that. Wylderide is strictly PC gaming. We're not going to consoles now, or ever if I have anything to do with it."

They had fought this battle many times, and it was just one more reason why she couldn't take him for a mate. He was a fantastic game designer, but his ambitions always outran their core philosophy as a gaming company—they would stick with the PC gamers who had always stuck with them, even in the early years when they were just a tiny startup before they were winning awards and getting featured in Wired magazine. If Brad were alpha and CEO of Wylderide, their games would be on Xbox, PlayStation, Wii U and even Nintendo, for Christ's sake.

Brad looked even more frustrated. "You have to think of the future, Nova. You're not the only person who works at Wylderide. We've got employees, now. People to think of—going to consoles will expand our market triple-fold."

"And betray everything we are to our current loyal customer base." She jabbed a finger at him. "Next thing you'll be saying we should add in-game purchases to *AfterPulse.*"

His jaw muscles worked. "Actually, I was thinking that if you *didn't* go for porting the games to Xbox, or one of the other consoles, that in-game purchases was the only way we were going to grow—"

Nova threw up her hands. "Oh for fuck's sake! Get out of my office." She turned her back on him and crossed her arms over her chest. Now he was just *trying* to piss her off.

Brad was silent for a second behind her. "Nova."

"What part of *get the fuck out* did you not understand?" Her rage was boiling over, even more than she normally felt when he suggested taking the company in a completely different direction than her father ever intended. Brad had fought endlessly with him over these issues, and now that he was gone… couldn't Brad see she was desperately trying to preserve her father's legacy? How could he not realize these things would be a complete betrayal of everything her father stood for?

She heard Brad move quietly behind her, then his hand landed at the small of her back. She flinched away and gave him a glare.

"You're right," he said.

"Damn straight, I'm right." She refused to look at him again.

"You're right that it's too soon to talk about this," he said softly. "I'm not going to say you're right about the business side of things, but you know what? I don't care. All I care about is you."

She let her head fall forward, the anger boiling off with his words. The truth was that Brad truly *did* care about her—she knew that—even if they fought like wolves and witches sometimes.

"Someday you're going to take a mate, Nova Wilding," he said softly at her back. "And when that day comes, I want it to be me."

And it always came back to that.

Brad and the other wolves… they were all waiting for her. She could feel it. The eyes that followed her every morning when she showed up for work. The whispers behind hands. She wouldn't be surprised if there were a company pool going about who she would pick. Only Brad had alpha-muscled his way to the front of the line, just like he always did. He'd been her father's favorite ever since he joined the pack five years ago. She'd only been a kid then, but Brad had always had his eye on her, she knew that.

And now… now fate had intervened and pushed the Question of Brad to the forefront. Now probably *was* exactly the right time to see if he was the alpha she could pledge her life to… and that Wylderide needed to move forward.

She just couldn't bring herself to do it.

"Nova," he said, voice still soft, conciliatory. "Let me take you to dinner. We'll start out slow, okay?" His warm fingers brushed the hair from the side of her neck. He leaned in, slipping an arm around her waist and holding her gently from behind.

She didn't resist.

He bent his head to whisper against her neck. "My wolf sings to you every night. All he dreams of is sinking his teeth into that beautiful neck of yours." Then his lips brushed her skin, sending gooseflesh racing across it. "You belong with me. You know you do. Let me in, and I'll make every fantasy you've ever had come true." Then he kissed her neck, only it was more of a nibble. He was feasting on her neck when she hadn't said so much as a word.

She cringed away from him and twisted forward, her

back to the city. Her hands went to his chest to shove him away, but he captured them and trapped them against him. He backed her against the glass.

"Stop pushing me away." His dark eyes bored into her, and he pressed one hand against the glass behind her head, leaning his body into hers. She could feel his erection straining through his pants, pressed into her side. "Do you see what you do to me? Stop fighting what you know is right. We belong together." Then he moved in to kiss her again... the hard feel of his hands on her, his body pressing her tight, his cock ready for her... it almost made her want to give in. To simply say, *yes, take me.* Claim me. Make all of it go away. It had been so long since she'd had a man, anyway...

But even as his lips fumbled around hers, she knew it was all wrong. Kissing Brad was like being swallowed by a hurricane, whereas kissing Owen...

She pushed Brad away and resisted the urge to wipe the residue of him off her mouth. Then she squirmed away from his hold and strode back to her desk. "I told you, I'm not ready."

The tense silence of his non-response spoke of his anger. She kept her head ducked, her hands busy tracing keys on her keyboard.

"I can wait, Nova." She could hear his breathing from across the room. "I've waited this long. But the pack can't wait, not forever. And I'm the right wolf for you—you know that."

She shook her head, still not looking at him. Not a definitive *no,* but one she hoped would at least get him the hell out of her office.

He stood there, waiting for an answer from her… then finally huffed his frustration and left, leaving the door propped wide.

Owen's scowl followed Brad as he marched away, then he turned an inscrutable expression to her through the open doorway. Heat rose in her face, and she hurried over to slam the door shut. Then she closed her eyes and leaned back against it.

Damn Brad and his demands. He didn't have a claim on her. No one did, not unless she chose it. And the mere fact that she could have Brad's lips on her while thinking thoughts about Owen… and how his kiss had charged her body like nothing she'd felt before… the whole idea of being with Brad, of giving up and giving in, turned to ash in her mouth.

Even her wolf agreed.

Kissing Owen was everything she wanted and

everything she could never have. And she liked it way too damn much for her own good.

Or the good of her father's company.

CHAPTER 3

It was late, going past ten o'clock, and Owen was pretty damn sick of sitting in his chair. He was waiting for Nova to finish out the day and come out of her office. But she was locked up tight and hadn't said a word all day to him. Owen hadn't heard a peep out of her since the throw down she had with that asshole Brad who works for her.

Owen was sure she hadn't eaten either, which was why he'd ordered up a sandwich to be delivered to the office. When it arrived, he decided it was time to drag her out and talk some sense into her, if not some dinner as well.

He tapped on her door and waited. There was no response. He knocked again, louder this time, and heard a muffled something through the door that he took as permission to enter.

Nova was buried behind her screen, her little form lost in that oversized black chair. Her arms were crossed in front of her chest, and headphones covered her ears. She stared at the screen, and the light of it flickered across her face.

She didn't even look up. "I said, go way." Her voice was way too loud with the headphones on. He wasn't entirely sure she was talking to him and not the screen.

He strolled up to the desk and dropped the bag of food next to her keyboard. She jerked back and gave it a strange look, as if she'd never seen take-out before. Then she tapped something rapidly on the keyboard, and the flickering stopped. She pulled her headphones off and set them on the desk.

Her cute, scrunched-up face peered up at him. "You brought me food?" As if that was the most unexpected thing he might do. Little did she know he'd been thinking of a whole lot of other *unexpected* things he could do with her—like bending her over that wide desk of hers. Or throwing her down on that rumpled cot she kept in the corner, obviously there for camping out late at night, working, like she was now. But those were thoughts to keep in his head, not spill out his mouth.

Instead, he shrugged one shoulder. "Unless you've got a secret snack bar in here, I figured you hadn't eaten all day." He glanced around the room for the tale-tell Doritos bags and Red Bull that a lot of coders at Wylderide used to decorate their desks, but hers was pristine. Just her keyboard, mouse, cell phone, headphones and… he finally caught a look at what was on her screen.

Shit. She was watching the video again—the one the hate group put up that listed all the names and locations of the Wilding pack. That video had tipped off whoever murdered her father and now was after her as well.

He shook his head at her. "Believe me, I understand losing yourself in work…" He flicked a hand at the screen. "But this is straight-up destructive what you're doing."

"It's not destructive," she protested, pushing back from the desk and rising to her feet.

He gave a non-committal *hmpf* and scrutinized the video, even though he'd seen it a hundred times. The star of the thing was a man in a metal-looking armor mask, like something a medieval knight would wear. It completely obscured his face. He called himself *The Wolf Hunter* in a modulated voice that made it untraceable— Owen and Riverwise had given it a shot, but came up with nothing. What was clear was the scrolling names and addresses of the wolves he had doxed—exposing them to a world that already hated shifters. But this was all old news, and there was nothing to be gained from her spending hours alone at night in her office going over it.

He dragged his gaze from the screen and back to her dark eyes, watching him… then he gestured to the video. "This isn't helping anyone—it's just going to tear you up some more."

She scowled at him. "I'm trying to figure out what we're really up against." Then she pursed her lips and turned away, marching to the window to stare out at the nightscape of the city.

She was dressed in one of those costumes again, the kind from her futuristic combat game. Most of the characters wore the same stylized black gear she had on the day before, but today, she was wearing a skimpy camouflage tank top, a pair of olive-drab cargo pants, and heavy black boots that probably weighed as much as she did. Her long black hair cascaded down her back, but he'd already noticed her perky little breasts holding their own under the tank. She wasn't wearing a bra as far as he could tell, and he shouldn't have noticed, but he did. He cursed himself for having thoughts like those when she was obviously still rattled by yesterday's attempt on her life. But that scorching hot kiss was still on his mind—in fact, it had played on an endless repeat throughout the day, as much as he tried not to let it.

She had her arms crossed with her back to him, clear across the room. He wanted to get closer, but she was the one who had moved away. And the way she had pushed him away in the medical warehouse still stung.

He stayed where he was. "I'm doing everything I can to keep you safe, Nova."

She unfolded her arms and glanced over her shoulder at him. "I know you are. That's about all I know anymore." Then she went back to looking out over the city.

It wasn't quite an invitation, but his body was getting squirrelly with so much distance between them. It was like she was a magnet, and while he didn't understand the source of it, he couldn't deny the pull. He kept his footfalls quiet as he stepped across the room.

"There's nothing for you to do about any of this tonight," he said softly, close at her back. "You need to knock off and go home. Some food wouldn't hurt you, either."

She turned to face him, and he didn't like the worry etched on her face. Then it twisted into a smirk. "Getting tired of babysitting me? Why, you got a hot date tonight?"

He dipped his chin to look her more steadily in the eyes. "No, ma'am." A sweet ache started up in the pit of his belly. The only hot date he wanted was standing in front of him.

He could see her react—lips part, eyes going a little more wide—then she broke the hot staring contest they were having and seemed to find something interesting to look at about mid-level in his chest. Or she was just avoiding looking in his eyes—he couldn't quite tell.

In almost a whisper, she said, "Brad wants me to be his mate."

"I'd already figured that much out for myself." He waited for more. If she wanted to open up to him, he would take all of that she wanted to give. It surprised him how much he craved it, too—almost as much as he wanted her lips on him again.

She finally brought her eyes up to meet his. "He just wants me for the business," she said, with more than a little bitterness. "Wylderide is worth a lot of money, but it's more than that—he wants to be alpha. He wants to lead the pack."

Owen eased a little closer to her. "So he's not just an asshole, he's a money hungry asshole."

She huffed a laugh but looked away. "He's not an asshole. I just don't want to be forced into picking him for a mate."

"That's easy enough—you tell him no." It seemed clear as day to him.

She turned those wide, dark eyes back to him. "It's not that easy. Wylderide's employees are almost all pack members—we have a few humans, awesome programmers who just want to hang in their cubicle coding all day and who don't mind being left out of pack affairs. But most of the company is my father's pack, and now they don't have an alpha. And they need one. Brad wants to be that alpha, and I can't lead the pack without a mate."

In one breath, she'd spilled more than she'd said to

him in all the time he'd known her.

He leaned in even closer, pressing a hand against the cool glass of the window behind her head. "But you don't want a mate," he said softly.

Her breathing picked up as he got closer, and he could feel his heart banging around in his chest.

"I don't want a mate that's just after my father's money." She kept glancing at his lips and letting her gaze flick down to his chest and back up again. She wanted him to kiss her, probably almost as much as he wanted to do the kissing.

He licked his lips. "I'm not looking for a mate. Can't have one, anyway. But I haven't been with a woman since I deployed last, and that was over two years ago. And here you are, prancing around in that tight tank top and loose combat pants, and can tell you this, darlin'—I definitely don't want you for your daddy's money."

Breath escaped her just as he leaned in for the kiss.

He started it, but she was a wildcat on him as soon as he did. Her hands shoved his jacket clear of his shoulders even as he was fighting to put his hands just about everywhere on her at once. She was small, and she tucked right into his chest as he devoured her lips, but the best part was how she moved against him, all hot and bothered and squirmy with his touch. He skimmed her hips and that little waist and round to her back to pull her close. When his fingers found the hem of her shirt and slipped inside, he couldn't help the moan. Her skin was hot and burning into his palm. Her whimper when he reached her breast about drove him insane. His cock was lost somewhere between them, but hard as a lighthouse making itself known.

She pulled away from his mouth enough to gasp, "Someone will hear us."

"Ain't no one here to listen," he panted against her neck. "You can go ahead and cry out all you like, baby girl." *God,* he was hard for her, and with her tight breast in one hand and her sweet ass in the other… it really had been forever, and he wasn't sure he would make it to the finish line with this rocket start they had going. But that didn't stop him from hooking her knee over his hip and making his intentions clear by driving his cock against her and pinning her to the window with his body.

They had entirely too many clothes on.

"We shouldn't," she gasped as he lifted her shirt above her breasts.

"I know." *Damn,* he could barely breathe to make words. "That's what makes it hot."

She moaned and shuddered against him. He lifted her arms above her head, holding them there with one hand so he could get her tank the hell off her body, but he stalled out when he got a good look at her perfect little breasts—just the size to cup his hand around, so he did.

"Goddamn, you're beautiful," he muttered as he went for the other with his mouth.

She gasped so loud, he almost didn't hear the phone go off behind him. He was too busy tasting her tight nipple and creamy flesh, but before he could come to his senses, she was squirming out of his arms...

And hurrying across the room, tugging her shirt down.

Dammit. She'd left him panting and aching again. He braced himself against the window as she scooped her phone off the desk.

"Hello?" Her voice was remarkably even for where he'd had her a moment ago.

It irked him something fierce.

"Brad, it's late," she huffed out, her back to Owen.

That irked him even more.

He growled and crossed the room, determined to rip that damn phone out of her hand and hang up on the asshole, but by the time he got there, she had the thing tucked between her ear and her shoulder, frowning as she tapped madly at her keyboard.

He huffed his frustration, standing behind her and running his hand through his hair instead.

Then what she brought up on the screen chilled him.

It was the Wolf Hunter again, only this time with more modern-looking metal-armor mask and a new video.

"Shit," she said under her breath. Then into the phone, "No, no, I've got it. Okay. No—I'll call you back." She hung up and set the phone down, then clicked the video to play.

Somehow the hate group got hold of a wolf. It was big. Maybe big enough to be a shifter. Owen couldn't tell, but *Jesus Christ,* the Wolf Hunter was dissecting the thing. Owen just gaped at it, horrified, as a step-by-step manual of instructions scrolled by on how to dispose of a wolf body.

A shifter body.

The video called on anyone who wanted to carry out the hate group's form of vigilante violence to be assured that this technique of body disposal would keep them clear of the law, since wolf DNA was different than human DNA. Which was true, but *fucking hell…* it was like one of those cooking videos on the internet, only a how-to manual for how to get away with murder.

Owen slammed his hand down on the keyboard, freezing the video.

Nova had sunk down into her chair, hand over her mouth, eyes wide in horror.

"Come on," he said, his voice rough. He tried to be gentle as he pulled her up out of her seat, but he wasn't brooking any nonsense from her. "I'm taking you home."

Fortunately, she didn't protest. In fact, he had to keep an arm around her the entire way to the elevator because it looked like her legs were about to give out. He was shaking, too, but with barely contained rage. *What the fuck* was that asshole thinking, calling her up and showing her that damn thing in the middle of the night? If he didn't have his hands full getting Nova home and safe, he'd hunt down Brad Hoffman and beat some sense into him.

Instead, he held a shaking Nova in his arms all the way down to her car.

CHAPTER 4

Nova had never been so cold in her life.

It wasn't the kind of cold that came from too much air conditioning in her car as Owen sped through the streets of Seattle, taking her home. Or the kind of chill that came from a harsh word, or a bad PR blitz for her game, or even the bitter loneliness as she stood over her father's grave bidding him a final goodbye. No, this was the kind of deep-in-her-bones cold that came from seeing a man carve up a wolf on a video and knowing, without question, that he meant for that to be *her*.

Her whole body shuddered for the hundredth time as Owen walked her up to her apartment in silence. His hand was on her elbow, keeping her steady, but also hurrying her along. Like it was a race to get her locked away in the high-rise, high-security condo Wylderide game money had bought for her. And she supposed it was. He probably wanted to tuck her away so he could finally go home for the night.

While Owen unlocked her door, she pulled out her phone to check the time. Her hand was shaking, but she could tell it was late. There were also a half dozen calls and texts from Brad, but those couldn't pierce the icy fog that was settling on her brain. She shoved the phone back in her pocket just as Owen latched onto her arm again and tugged her inside.

He closed the door, locked it, and parked her next to it. "Wait here," he said with dark, serious eyes peering deep into hers.

She nodded.

He whisked away. *What was he doing?* She watched dully as he hurried through her apartment, closing the blinds, checking the kitchen, running to the back bedroom, then circling around again to inspect the living area. She didn't know what he was doing until he stopped dead-center in the room, squeezing his eyes shut and running his hand through his hair.

Then she realized: he was checking for something, or someone, that might kill her.

That deep-body-cold gripped her again, like an open grave was waiting for her. The full-body shudder slumped her back against the door. It was graceless, and the thump drew Owen's attention again. He dropped his hand from his hair and hurried over. She tried to scoot out of the way so he could open the door to leave, but she didn't get far—her legs were shaking too much.

"Sorry," she said, ducking and bracing herself against the wall. She blinked at her hand pressed against it, knowing she should move, but somehow held transfixed by the coolness of the plaster on her palm. "I know you want to get going," she said, thickly, not looking at him. "I guess I'll… I'll see you in the morning." She slowly dragged her gaze up to his.

His brow was wrinkled like he was puzzled by something. "I'm not going anywhere." His voice was rough. "I'm staying here to make sure you're safe. You've got a couch that will suit just fine."

He was staying. The relief that washed through her

suddenly turned her legs weak, and she sagged against the wall that was holding her up. His arms were around her in an instant, warm and strong and lifting her away from the wall.

"Hey, now," he said, words soft but his arms strong around her. "You're okay. I'm not letting anything hurt you."

She clung to him, her arms going automatically around his neck, her face burying in his shoulder. "Oh, God, Owen, that video…"

"You forget about that video." Some edge had come back to his voice.

"I can't, I just…" Her body shuddered again, and she clutched him tighter. "Hold me."

"I'm holding you." His hands moved to lay flat against her back, and somehow that was better.

She bunched the back of his collar in her hands. "Tighter."

"I've got you," he whispered into her hair. His hands pressed her shaking body into his hard-muscled one, and that chased away some of the chill. In fact, the way his fingers were kneading the muscles of her back and working into her hair… it was lighting a fire inside her that burned low in her belly. She released her clutching of his clothes and slid her hands up into the short military buzz of his hair.

"Owen," she gasped, her heart rate starting to pick up.

His head dipped down to her. "Hush." His lips moved against her forehead. "You don't say anything. I know just what you need."

Then he tipped her head back, and his lips found hers. They were gentle at first, barely a brush against her, but it surged the fire inside her even brighter. Suddenly she was pulling him down for a deeper kiss like he was the air she needed to keep breathing. He dove in, his hands clutching at her as much as she was grabbing hold of him, their tongues battling for dominance. His hands were everywhere—cupping her bottom, sliding down over her hip, up between their bodies to grasp her breast through her shirt. His rough squeeze made her whimper, and she was hot with need. He groaned and pushed her back against the door, pinning her while he owned her mouth. His hand was under her shirt now, warm palm on her breast, fingers twisting her nipple and making her cry out—not with pain but with the firestorm he was creating inside her, burning away all thoughts and fears and that deep, dark chill. There was nothing but Owen's mouth on her neck, feasting on her as he slipped his hand down the front of her pants. Breath huffed out of her body as his fingers dove straight to her most sensitive parts. But he only tormented her with the promise of pleasure, snatching his hand back out to lift her tank top free of her body in one swipe. Then both his hands slipped down the back of her pants, his mouth working a hot line of biting kisses down her front as he dropped to his knees, taking her clothes with him.

She braced herself on his shoulders as she stepped out of her boots and pants, and the moment she was free— completely naked now against the door—he lifted her knee over his shoulder and dove into her sex, tongue first. She melted with the hot feel of his mouth on her, then his fingers soon followed, thrusting roughly inside her and blasting her toward an orgasm that felt like an oncoming avalanche. She banged her head back against the door as it rocked her body. She bucked into him, but he held her tight, fingers of one hand digging into her hip while she convulsed around the other ones thrusting deep inside her. Just as the wave peaked, he curled his fingers, hitting a spot that had her crying out and bucking against him again.

She was dizzy with it as he left her body, leaving her suspended against the door in a haze of pleasure while he tore off his shirt and shoved down his pants. She only got a momentary look at his cock—hard and mouth-wateringly large and ready for her—before he was on her again. She moaned as the hot skin of his chest pressed her into the door. His hands lifted her bottom, and suddenly she was off her feet. He wrapped her legs around his waist, and she grabbed hold of his broad shoulders just as he thrust that hot cock inside her. She screamed his name, and he let loose a guttural growl that pulsed waves of pleasure through her with every thrust. He had her pinned hard against the door, owning her body, releasing her from the world as she floated higher on every door-rattling pound.

"Nova." It was a warning, a growl, and a fiercely possessive sound, all in one word. "Come for me." He leaned into the crook at her neck and bit her—not a claiming bite with fangs, just his human teeth claiming pleasure from her—but it was enough to send her over the edge.

"Owen." She gasped and then came undone. Giant, throbbing waves of pleasure wrecked her. Owen kept thrusting inside her through the rise and fall of the waves until he let loose his own growling-hoarse grunt of pleasure, his rock-hard body shuddering against hers. She

could feel his release shooting hot inside her.

He slowed his pace, still moving against and inside her, and his mouth on her neck gentled. Then he eased her to the floor, pulling out of her body, and yet leaving her filled with pleasure. He nipped bites all over her chest and belly and down to her sex, cupping his hot hand against the throbbing wetness there. She moaned with the after-pleasure he was giving her, gentle and hot. He rose up to hold her again, and she fairly slumped against him, weak with pleasure.

He took a second to hike up his pants, then without a word, he reached down, hooked his arm under the backs of her knees, and lifted her up. He carried her like that through the apartment, and her eyes slid shut of their own accord. She was so tired, so limp from their hot sex against the door, that she didn't even murmur a question of where they were going. When she lazily opened them again, they were in her bedroom. Owen gently set a knee down on the bed, then placed her on it. He drew back the covers and scooped her up again only to slide her underneath them. The sheets were cool against her hot skin, but it was a pleasure-filled coolness this time. She expected him to crawl in with her, but he just pulled the covers up to her neck and kissed her forehead—like she was a child he was tucking in for the night.

"Sleep, Mistress NovaCaine," he whispered and gave her a small smile along with a tender look that reached straight inside her.

She grabbed at his arm as he pulled away. "Where are you going?"

He stroked her hand clutching onto him. "I won't be far. Just to the couch. I promise."

"Don't leave." She wanted him in her bed. It seemed wrong for him to be anywhere else.

He smiled and dipped back down to kiss her tenderly on the lips. "If I sleep in here, no actual sleeping is going to get done. And you need to rest."

He kissed her forehead again and drew back fast enough that she couldn't catch him. And she was too tired, too worn out from the world and the sex and everything, to chase after him. She slumped back into the pillow and watched him go through half-lidded eyes.

She tried to keep them open, but they slid shut as he closed her bedroom door.

Her last thought before drifting off was a vague idea that Owen wanted the couch because it was closer to the front door.

He was keeping her *safe*, even now… just as he promised.

CHAPTER 5

Owen awoke on Nova's couch.

It took him a moment to sort how that happened. His mind was definitely still thinking about pressing her smokin' little body up against the door, having some of the hottest sex he'd ever had. In fact, his body was still there, too—he had a raging hard-on even before he blinked open his eyes to the morning sun. For a moment, he lay there, hand on his cock, thinking about her and getting his bearings. She was asleep in the bedroom, right where he left her, and the door was closed. If she came out now, he'd be hard-pressed not to back her right into the bedroom, throw her on the bed, and work off his erection that way.

But that wasn't what Nova Wilding needed from him.

Which was why he was on the couch, far from the temptation of her sweet, sweet body.

No. He needed to get some breakfast going and come up with a plan to deal with this Wolf Hunter. Last night, Owen had been focused on getting Nova to safety and calming her down. But now in the bright light of morning, he needed a better plan than just relieving the insane sexual tension that was still tenting out his pants.

There was nothing wrong with taking Nova hard and fast against the door. In fact, there were all kinds of right about it. She'd really needed something at that moment, something he was more than willing to give—comfort; the security of someone looking out for her; and a hot distraction to take her mind off the danger.

But she had stirred something more than just his cock last night. Normally, he would say his wolf was calling for her—but this was something different. Something primal, untamed, and very deep inside him. It surged up whenever he kissed her, much less sunk his cock deep inside her hot little body. She was bringing something out of him. Something that should most likely stay buried.

Nova wasn't looking for a mate, anyway, at least not from him. Which was just as well, because claiming a mate meant shifting and that wasn't happening. He'd told her the truth about that. No, he needed to keep his cock and whatever was raging deep inside him under better control. Otherwise, he might be more of a danger to her than the Wolf Hunter.

Owen tossed off the small throw that had been his blanket and stretched out his sex-sore muscles on the way to the kitchen. His dress pants were still loose around him, not entirely zipped from the night before, and his cock was still tenting them out. He rubbed his eyes and tried to think of mundane things to tame his erection. He got the coffee pot going. He found the plates and pans for rustling up some breakfast.

Nothing was working.

As he sorted through the refrigerator, pulling out eggs and milk and butter, his mind kept drifting back to last night. The scent of their encounter hung in the air, and that wasn't helping. His body knew she was sleeping in the next room, just waiting for him. He set the breakfast supplies on the counter and let out a growl of frustration. Then he yanked open the refrigerator door, grabbed a

Coke, and held it against his crotch.

Fuck, that was cold. He squeezed eyes tight against it, gritting his teeth, but keeping the Coke in place, until he was sure his blood flow had been permanently chilled.

"You okay?" The voice startled him, and he convulsed in front of the open refrigerator, popping open his eyes and yanking the Coke away from his crotch.

Nova stood in front of him in a long T-shirt that barely covered her ass. Her bed-head hair was all mussed and sticking up, her head was cocked to the side, and she was squinting at him. *Sexy as all hell.*

"Don't sneak up on me like that." He coughed. *Unbelievable.* He'd been caught with a Coke on his cock. Then again, he wasn't entirely sure she'd noticed.

She gave him a lazy, sexy smile. "Aren't you the security guy? I shouldn't be able to sneak up on you, should I?"

He closed the refrigerator door and held the Coke up like he had planned all along to pull that out for breakfast. Then he wagged a finger at her. "That's right. And I've been thinking—we need a more secure location for you to stay."

She frowned, but she didn't seem to grasp what he was saying. "That sounds suspiciously like a decision that requires my brain to function. I require coffee first."

He smirked. "Just so happens I've got some brewing." He grabbed a mug out of the cabinet, poured her a cup, and then set it on the small breakfast table. She went to it like a starving man goes to a feast, then cradled the cup in her hands and held it up to her face to breathe it in. That look on her face was doing things to his cock again.

He turned away and started making breakfast.

She moaned, drawing his attention back from the crackling and popping of the scrambled eggs in the pan. He gave her a questioning look.

"I am *famished*," she said, hungrily eyeing the pan.

"Breakfast coming right up." He finished the eggs and dished them out. When he brought them to the table, the steam wafted across her face, and she breathed that in, too.

He sat down across from her. Her dark eyes were starting to open more fully, but she was still in that short T-shirt with the mussed hair. She looked too damn good. He could see his way to waking up to that sight every morning.

What the hell? He evicted that thought and kicked its ass on the way out.

Then he scooped a mouthful of eggs into his mouth.

"So, as I was saying—"

She held up a finger to stop him, then raked her eyes over his half-dressed body, making him acutely aware that he hadn't bothered to put on a shirt.

"You know," she said with a dead-sexy smile, "you really can't sit there half dressed, feeding me eggs and coffee, and expect me to forget what happened last night."

He swallowed his eggs and smirked. "I *was* aiming for unforgettable."

Her smokin' hot look in return had him aching to drag her off to bed. He coughed into his hand again and dug his fork into the eggs. "But we really need to talk about what's happening next."

She leaned back from her plate, studying him. "Did we, or did we not, have raging hot sex last night?"

He met her gaze. "We did."

She leaned forward, looking him over again. "Are we, or are we not, going to do that again?"

He smiled. "I couldn't say. That's up to you, Ms. Wilding."

She nodded and bit her lip, looking thoughtful. "This is just between you and me. No one else needs to know, right?"

If that Coke had been pressed to his cock again, he couldn't have chilled any faster.

"I suppose that's right." It shouldn't bother him that she only wanted a casual fuck... but it did. It should bother him even less that she wanted to keep it a secret—after all, Riverwise wasn't going to give him an award for seducing his client—but it *did* bother him. A lot.

Owen got up and carried his plate to the sink, scraping out the rest of the eggs, given his appetite had suddenly taken a vacation. Why was he so worked up? He needed to do his damn job and keep her safe—the rest of it was just trouble waiting to happen.

He turned back to her. "What matters is where you're going to stay. I promised I'd keep you safe, and I aim to do that. It's why I'm here."

She was frowning and biting her lip some more. "Thank you."

And like *that* he was back to wanting to haul her off to the bedroom. "It's just common sense to move you back to the River brothers' safehouse."

She shook her head. "I'm not running off to the mountains over this, Owen. *I can't.* I've got a business to run, and we're about to release the beta. This is the biggest launch we've had in years, and that safehouse is what? An hour away? I can't be commuting back and forth like that—"

He lurched back to the table. "So you prefer being dead?"

She rolled her eyes.

He reached across the table and grabbed her hand. It was soft and warm and small inside his hold, and for the first time, all the anger and the urgency and the heavy need for her fled, leaving behind just a naked fear. That she wouldn't take this seriously… and *that* would end up with her dead.

"Nova, *please.*" He was begging now. "This Wolf Hunter could just be some lunatic… or he could be stirring up dozens of vigilantes. He's calling for every nutjob in the state to go after shifters. Specifically Wilding pack shifters. Very specifically your father… and *you.* We've got to use our heads about this."

She pulled her hand away from his, but not before giving him a little squeeze. "I'm not the only Wilding he's targeting. Sure, there's been an attack on my father and myself, but all of the Wilding pack, including all my employees at Wylderide, are at risk. What kind of message does it send if I go hiding out in the mountains while leaving it to all of them to keep my father's business on the rails?"

He scowled. "You'll give them the message that you have a brain in your head."

A storm took over her face. "I have plenty of brains in my head. Enough to know that I don't have to sit here and argue with you." She rose up from her seat. "I'm taking a shower. And then I'm going to work. If you want to be my bodyguard, you can come along."

She stomped off to her bedroom and slammed the door behind her.

Owen dropped into his chair, then plopped his head into his hands. Could he possibly have fucked that up any more?

He shoved his way up from the chair again, poured himself a cup of coffee, and slugged it down. The truth was, she *was* smart. And brave. She'd been shook, sure, but a lesser woman would have fallen apart under the circumstances. Unfortunately, smarts and bravery didn't always add up to a sense of self-preservation. Add in a huge helping of Wilding-flavored stubbornness, and Owen had no idea how he was going to keep her from getting herself killed.

But really, all of that didn't matter. It was his job to

keep her safe. He'd just have to find a way to do it, regardless.

CHAPTER 6

Nova had her battle gear on in more ways than one.

She stomped into the Wylderide office in her special ops gear uniform from the upcoming release of *Domination: AfterPulse.* She'd worn the custom outfit before, but it was relatively new, so she still caught some glances on the way in. But the curious faces quickly ducked down below their cubicle walls when they saw the storm brewing on her face.

Goddamn Owen.

The man was driving her insane… and also following her like a shadow, silent and three steps behind, as she marched through the office. He was overprotective and insanely hot, but that crack about her not being smart about this threat from the Wolf Hunter… she wanted to fire his ass and send him packing back to Riverwise.

Only she needed him.

And not just because her lady parts were still happily sore from their wild sex against her front door. She needed his protection to make sure she didn't actually do something stupid with this. Because the truth was, she was terrified… the terror had nearly made her collapse the night before. It was only Owen's steady, commanding care—not to mention the hot sex—that had gotten her through it.

I know just what you need.

His words still made her hot. And frustrated. And want to ball up her fists and pound on something. Because he was asking her to drop everything and run off to some secret hideaway in the mountains that the River pack kept. The three River pack brothers who ran Riverwise, the private security company Owen worked for, had done a lot of great things for the Wilding pack, and she was sure they would welcome her—the problem was exactly as she told Owen.

She had a company to run.

Nova made a bee-line for her office. She stopped at the door and turned to face Owen behind her. His expression was still set on Stony Scowl Mode. He'd been silent ever since they had fought in her kitchen earlier this morning. She could see his jaw muscles flex, but he said nothing.

She glared at him, then wrenched open her door and fled inside. She managed to not slam the door, but once it was shut, and Owen and his hot scowl were outside, she slumped against the door and wondered what on earth she was doing.

She didn't *want* to fight with him. He'd been nothing but kind to her before the crack about her brains, or lack thereof. And she knew almost nothing about him except that he'd saved her life and her sanity once apiece this week already. She shouldn't be so ticked off by one comment. She shouldn't *care* about him at all. Sure, he was insanely hot and the sex was scorching, but it wasn't like she planned to take him for a mate. Which only made her think about that cryptic comment he made when he had her up against the office window—*can't have a mate, anyway*. Who *was* this Owen character? Why couldn't he have a mate? And how did he slip under her skin so easily?

She jumped when someone pounded on the door she was leaned against and just barely got out of the way before it shoved open.

It was Brad.

Great. She stepped back and just caught the look of fury on Owen's face before Brad shut the door.

"Nova," Brad breathed out as he pulled her into his arms. He held her tight. Too tight.

She struggled to get out of his hold, and it took him a moment to release her.

"Jesus, girl, you can't just not answer your phone like that!" He frowned as she backed several steps away. "What's wrong?"

"I'm under no obligation to return your calls." God, she was fuming at Brad now, too. What was wrong with her?

"I was *worried* about you." His scrunched-up expression looked hurt. Then he glanced back at the closed door. "What's going on with the bodyguard? He's more of a pain in the ass than normal. Do you want me to get rid of him? Because I'd like to do that anyway."

Nova rubbed a hand across her forehead. "No, it's not

Owen's fault. Well, it *is,* but…" Oh, God, what a mess. "He annoys me sometimes, but he's just doing his job."

Brad stepped toward her. "There are other bodyguards. You're under enough stress as it is, you don't need this asshole—"

"No!" It came out too harsh. She reined it in. "Owen stays. He… took care of me last night. He stayed over."

Brad's eyes went a little wider, then he looked her over.

She didn't like his scrutiny, so she turned away and strode to her desk. "What do you want, Brad?"

"The bodyguard *stayed over?"* he asked, brow furrowed.

Shit. "Yes, he stayed over. I was scared, all right? That video freaked me out." She kept her head down, tapping open her screen and pulling up her email. Maybe if she ignored him, he would go away.

He didn't. Brad strode to her desk, then braced his hands on it, leaning across it and forcing her to look at him. "You fucked the bodyguard," he said with wide eyes like he could hardly believe it.

"Oh, for God's sake!"

"You *did.*" There was amazement in his voice, then a dark storm gathered on his face.

She shoved a finger at him. "It is none of your

business who I sleep with!"

Seventeen emotions crossed Brad's face before he finally settled on a deep scowl. "You and I both know that's not true." His voice was deadly calm, and that was what unsettled her the most. "Tell me he didn't claim you."

"*What?* Jesus, Brad."

"Tell me." His face was stone cold.

"He did not claim me. *God.*"

"I want him out of your apartment. And out of Wylderide." His voice was icy with determination. "Today."

She gave him a *what the fuck?* shake of her head, speechless for a moment. "What makes you think you can tell me what to do? *I'm* the boss around here. *I'm* the alpha's daughter. So how about you get your subversive ass out of my office before I fire you?" She swept a hand toward the door.

But he didn't. He bit his lip, stared at the carpet, then slowly came around her desk to face her. "You're the boss, Nova—on the game, in the office, all of it. But not the pack. And you *know* that. I made a vow to look after you like your father would—because I was his beta, and that's what betas do. You *know* I want you. You've known that for… well, ever since you were old enough to figure it out. Maybe you don't want me. Maybe you'll pick someone else. But for God's sake, Nova, don't pick someone outside the pack."

Her shoulders slumped, and she couldn't look him in the face. Because he was right. Mating outside the pack would tear it apart—and Wylderide with it. It was the opposite of what she was supposed to be doing.

She just shook her head. Tears she didn't want came unbidden to her eyes.

Brad's hand slid across her shoulder to gently rub the back of her neck. "I know you're scared. I couldn't sleep last night, I was so worried about you. But this whole Wolf Hunter thing has to blow over soon. Until then, please, Nova, just lie low—"

"I'm not going to hide up in the mountains!" She shoved his hand off.

"The mountains?" Brad's brow wrinkled up in confusion.

"Owen wants me to run off to Riverwise's safehouse."

Brad scowled. "I'm sure he does."

"It's not like that," she growled. But then she thought of doing exactly that—running off with Owen and hiding out in the mountains, secluded, just her and Owen's hot body. A flush ran through her, and she was shocked how much she yearned for that fantasy to come true—to leave everything, all her responsibilities, behind and play with a sexy shifter. It was completely irresponsible, and that was probably why she ached for it. She sucked in a breath and pushed that thought aside. "Owen wants me to stay away from E3 next week, as well as the Finals Tournament in a couple days—"

"E3 is an enormous conference, Nova." He looked aghast. "You can't go to that. That's insane!"

She heaved a sigh. "I have to go."

"You do *not* have to go. Nova, *think*. Your father was murdered at a con. The grenade attack came at the VA. Not here at the Wylderide. Not at your apartment. It's when you're out in the world that you're most at risk. We should double up on guards here, where it's hardest for anyone to get to you in the first place, then keep you away from the public for a while."

"Have you forgotten we're releasing the beta in just over a week?" she complained.

"So? It can release without an executive rep from Wylderide out on the PR circuit. The world will not end."

"I'm *not* going to let this Wolf Hunter stop me from fulfilling my father's dreams!" There, she finally said it.

Tears glassed her eyes, so she turned away, wrapping her arms tight around her chest.

Brad was quiet. Then he came up behind her and gently held her shoulders. "I miss him, too," he said softly.

As hard as she tried to keep it in, a small sob escaped her. God, she was an emotional wreck. Losing her father and his steady hand on the business and her life… the threats from the Wolf Hunter… her sexy bodyguard sweeping her into his arms… all of it had unmoored her from her normal, steady, calm existence. The one where she coded and played games and at most worried about whether she actually loved Brad Hoffman or if she could mate with him even if she didn't.

Brad's warm hands squeezed her shoulders a little. "Losing your father was a blow to everyone at Wylderide. They can't afford to lose you, too, Nova."

She knew he was speaking as much about himself as the rest of the pack, but it was true—everyone was carrying on in her father's name, in spite of the threats. If something happened to her… everything would fall apart.

She gave Brad a nod without speaking or turning, still trying to beat back the tears.

"A compromise, then," he said calmly. "You stay away from the conference because there's just no way to make that secure. You make a brief appearance at the tournament to give it your blessing and to congratulate the teams. Then you lay low until the beta is released. And we double guards everywhere."

She sucked in a breath and finally turned to face him. "All right. On the condition that I keep Owen."

Brad winced but didn't protest.

"As my bodyguard," she clarified. It truly wasn't his business who she slept with—until she chose a mate, she was free to shop around and be with whomever she wanted. He knew that. Even more, he knew her well enough to tell she was drawing a line he better not cross.

"If that's what you want." But he wasn't happy about it.

"It is."

He nodded and turned to leave. When he opened the door, she could see Owen's attention snap to it, a glare ready for Brad as he came out.

Brad hesitated on the threshold. "I came in here to check on you, but I also wanted to tell you the VA sent a note of thanks. The soldiers have apparently all been volunteering for guard duty for you, ever since they found out what happened in the grenade attack." He gave her a small smile. "You have a lot of fans."

She laughed a little, but her chest hurt. It must have shown on her face because Brad left the doorway to come back and hug her. It was warm and friendly and lasted a bit too long. Then he cupped her cheeks, kissed her forehead, and whispered, "We're going to get through this, I promise."

She nodded and managed to beat back her tears.

Brad gave her a smile, then strolled from the office. It wasn't until he was gone—and she saw Owen's ice-coated glare trailing after him—that she realized Brad had carefully orchestrated that whole little show for Owen to watch through the open door.

Her face flamed hot. Damn men marking their territory! She strode toward the door, and just as Owen sprung up to his feet like he had finally decided to talk, she closed it in his face.

CHAPTER 7

Owen was driving Nova's personal car up the winding mountain roads to the Riverwise safehouse. The natural beauty of the Olympic forest provided fantastic scenery—and Nova Wilding in the seat next to him in her futuristic battle gear outfit was easy on the eyes as well—if it weren't for that scowl on her face.

"We're not staying, right?" she asked for the second time. "I just want to make sure we're clear on that."

"Clear as a bell," Owen said with a grimace. "If it

doesn't trouble you too much, I'd like to stay for more than five minutes. Might take me that long to round up some clothes, not to mention a toothbrush. I may be camping out at your apartment, but I'd rather not smell like it. Living in the same clothes is something I left behind with the Army." Not to mention that he'd spent a year in that state while being experimented on. A change of clothes was a mental necessity for him these days. "And I aim to check in with the River brothers if they're available. They are my bosses."

Jace, Jaxson, and Jared were about as far from being tyrant bosses as he was from being a spring lily, but Owen was genuinely hoping to get hold of Jace—he had questions his former brother-in-arms was uniquely suited to answer, given he was mated to a Wilding female.

Nova didn't reply, just went back to scowling at the trees as they whizzed past. They'd almost reached the mountain estate. It was a huge enterprise governed by the matriarch of the River family—she'd been amazingly kind and motherly to everyone who walked in the door, including him. Dozens of shifters had taken up residence, some who'd been captured and didn't have homes to return to, like Owen, and some who just needed a safe place to stay until this government business of kidnapping shifters off the streets had been stopped. Once that had been accomplished, many of them were sticking around due to the hate group threats. And to help Mama River run the safehouse, which was a sprawling ranch.

Even though a few members of the Wilding pack had opted to stay at the safehouse until they got this hate group business sorted, Owen had barely been able to drag Nova up here. But he couldn't just take off to run up here and get some things—he was determined not to let her out of his sight, regardless of whether she was pissed off at him. Or not. Or wanted to take him to bed. Or not. Somehow those things were really mixed up. Or at least they seem to be for her.

For him, too, if he was honest.

But the necessity of a change of clothes was real, and eventually, she relented. It was that, or get a new bodyguard, and she didn't seem to want someone else watching over her. At least, he hadn't driven her off yet by opening his stupid mouth again. Which was a good thing because, even if she ordered him away, he wasn't sure he would go.

"I hear Terra Wilding is staying at the safehouse," Owen said, trying to sound casual. "So, if you decided to relocate temporarily, at least you'd have one of your cousins nearby."

She scowled those pretty, dark eyes at him. "If you're going to spend this whole time trying to talk me into staying up here—"

Owen lifted one hand from the steering wheel, a sign of surrender. "I'm just saying. You Wildings could do worse than get together as a family. I figured that was something you'd like to do anyway. Maybe I was wrong about that." He didn't really understand the Wilding pack. Where he came from, most packs stuck together... and they kept to one family business. His father's pack ran the Harding ranch. The River pack were all ex-military and employees for Riverwise, the private security company that Owen worked for now. When he'd taken the job, he'd also joined the pack, pledging his submission to Jaxson River, the pack alpha. And Owen had been happy to do so—the River brothers had saved his life. Plus that was just how most pack-run companies operated. Either you were all-in or you were out.

But the Wildings were different.

True to their name, they seemed a lot more independent than most shifters. The list of Wilding names posted by the Wolf Hunter showed they were scattered, not just across Seattle, but all over the world. Nova's family-run gaming business was a bit of an exception within the sprawling Wilding family. They were clearly a pack—although Nova had mentioned some of the employees were human—and it came with the usual pack politics. They had all sworn submission to Nova's father as alpha... at least, until he was murdered. And now her father's beta, Brad, obviously had his eye on the alpha's daughter for his mate. Owen had stepped into the middle of that, and he knew from his pack back home, that an outsider in the middle of pack politics was no place to be.

But it didn't stop him from wanting to be by her side 24/7 either.

Nova was back to staring out the window. "My cousin Terra puts the *wild* in Wilding." She gave him a sideways look. "You might think I'm crazy for not wanting to stay at the safehouse, but I'm frankly stunned that someone talked Terra into it."

Owen shrugged one shoulder. "From what I hear, her little sister was kidnapped by the same assholes who experimented on me. That's the sort of thing that puts the fear of God into most normal people."

He gave her a meaningful look, implying that perhaps

a little fear would be a good thing for her, but her dark eyes just burned with unspoken words. He was sure she was cursing him in her head again.

Time to change subjects, before he yanked her clear off the chain. "What's the story with the Wilding family structure, anyhow? Seems like ya'll are spread out all over. How'd that come to be?"

Nova sucked in a breath, but when she looked at him again, some of that burning anger was gone. "Our family spread out for a reason, but that reason goes back two generations. It's only now, in my generation of cousins, that we're starting to get over it. Somewhat."

"Some kind of blood feud, then?" That he knew something about. Small-town Texas feuds could get intense. That was part of why he got the hell out. He was never much for that kind of drama.

Nova nodded, solemnly. "Back in my grandfather's generation, the Wildings were one large, sprawling family pack. There were two brothers at the head of it—one was alpha, and one was beta. Together, they had a pack that was probably a hundred wolves strong, many of them cousins and brothers and relatives. But Gary and Bobby ruled them all. Gary was alpha, but everything went sideways and bloody when he found out Bobby was, well, spending a little too much time with Gary's mate."

"Holy shit." Owen was aghast. "You are kidding me."

Nova pinked up a little in the cheeks. "Nope. It's pretty much the secret family shame. You probably think even worse of us Wildings now."

"Hey, now." He peered at her. "I don't judge folks by their relatives." He certainly couldn't claim to have a fine pedigree back home, that was for sure. "But a beta cheating with the alpha's mate? How does that even happen?" He couldn't picture it. Betas were sworn to their alphas—it was virtually impossible to go against their alpha's command. The magic of the bond was just too strong. And to sin against a brother as well...

Nova shook her head "I don't know. There are all kinds of rumors about it. That Bobby wasn't really a wolf—that he was some kind of male witch instead. Or that he was a white wolf."

"White wolf?" Owen frowned. "The only white wolf I've ever seen was Grace Krepky." She was Jared River's mate and currently campaigning to be the first openly-shifter member of Congress.

"Me, too," Nova said. "And I don't know what her story is, but before a month ago, I'd have told you white wolves were just legend, in spite of the Wilding pack rumors. Now I'm not so sure. Regardless, the thing that really tore the pack apart was the possibility that some of Gary's pups were actually Bobby's. No one really knows, because when Gary found out that Bobby had been sleeping with his mate, all hell broke loose. A lot of wolves died that day, including Gary and his mate."

"Wait… you mean *the beta* survived?" Owen couldn't even imagine it. "How did Gary's pack not tear that guy apart? He violated every pack rule that ever existed, not to mention committing acts of indecency against his fellow wolves and brothers."

"Which is why they thought he was a witch." Nova shook her head. "I have no idea how, but Bobby escaped. As you can imagine, none of the pups were too eager to be identified as possibly half witch, so they weren't too excited to run after him. Not to mention they were all kids at the time. In the end, everyone who could hold the pack together was either dead or gone. The whole thing fell apart, scattered to the winds."

"So how does your pack fit into that pile of snakes?" Owen was amazed that any of them would talk to the others *at all* after that kind of history.

"My father's generation were Gary's pups. Each was suspicious of the others not being a true son of Gary

Wilding. Once they scattered and separated, the five brothers formed the five dominant Wilding families in the area. My father, Arthur, and the four brothers—Astor, Donnie, Frank, and Billy. Astor you might've heard of—he's Colonel Astor Wilding, Piper's father."

Oh, Owen definitely knew who Colonel Astor Wilding was. He was the one responsible for Owen losing a year of his life to a cage. And losing his wolf and himself in a haze of genetic experimentation. The man was straight-up evil—he'd even imprisoned his own sons, Noah and Daniel. "Yeah, I'd lay money on that one being spawned from the Bobby Wilding strain of the family."

Nova scowled. "I'm glad the Colonel is under arrest for his part in what happened to you. And the other wolves. That was some terrible business. But Jace's mate, Piper, and her brothers are decent people. I think. I don't really know them too well."

"So which brother is Terra's father?" Owen was trying to get this whole Wilding family tree solid in his mind, but it was a lot to track.

"Terra's father is Donnie Wilding. She's got a brother Trent, and you know about her little sister, Cassie, the one who was kidnapped. Terra's a little crazy—she's an artist—but it's not like we're enemies. We even had her shoot some concept pictures for *Domination*. She does urban photography, and we were looking for a future-urban cityscape kind of look."

Owen nodded—maybe this Terra cousin would be a way to convince Nova she needed to stay at the safehouse. "Maybe you and Terra can catch up while I talked to Jace about some business." The business was *her*, but he wasn't going to say that.

Nova scowled at him. "Just don't take too long. I've got a lot of prep for the tournament, still."

"Yes, ma'am." He smiled, a genuine one for the first time since the morning. At least they were talking again, instead of the constant, stony silence.

They were finally pulling up to the ranch. The parking lot was filled with cars, as it had been ever since Owen made this his new home. After Jace had sprung him, there was no way in hell he was going back to the Army, but he didn't have money or a place to stay, either. Like many of the liberated shifters, Mama River had been kind enough to take him in. He'd just need to grab a few things, talk with Jace about the sticky situation with Nova, and get her back to her apartment, if that's the way it was going to be. If he were lucky, her cousin would talk her into staying. Owen had played all his cards with that.

After they parked and strode in the front door—the place was huge, so knocking was usually pointless—Owen brought Nova to the oversized kitchen. A frantic bustle was underway, getting ready for the dinner hour for the hordes. Owen gave a small wave to Mama River, who was ordering people about.

"Don't let those potatoes cook too long," she said to one of the shifters manning the stovetop. Then she quickly ushered them into the adjoining dining room.

She brushed her long, gray hair back over her shoulder, then gave Nova a look-over that made heat rush to Owen's face. She turned back to him. "Owen Harding, so this is what's been keeping you busy."

He didn't want her jumping to conclusions—even if they were the correct conclusions—so he rushed out, "Just doing my duty, ma'am."

Mama River hiked up her eyebrows but kept the smile. "Well, that's unfortunate. And excuse my manners, Nova Wilding. Welcome to my home! I was just hopeful that our Owen had found a mate. I've had a run of luck on that lately."

Owen smiled, but it was a bit forced. Mama Wilding could put some southern ladies to shame with her full-court press to find mates for every young wolf under her roof. "Finding a mate isn't exactly on my radar right now, Mama River. But I do need to talk to Jace about the business of keeping our Wilding pack friends safe."

She tipped her head toward the kitchen. "Last I saw, he was out back, instructing some of our new guests on tending the horses."

"If it's not too much trouble, could you look after Nova for a bit? I hear her cousin's staying at the estate?"

Nova gave him a slightly wide-eyed look. "Maybe I should come with you."

Mama River looked between the two of them and came to his rescue. "Actually, Nova, I could use your help. Terra's got her eyes set on redecorating her room. Maybe you can help me convince her that's unnecessary." Mrs. River took Nova by the elbow and steered her away from the kitchen.

Nova threw a scowl back over her shoulder, and Owen couldn't help the wide grin that broke across his face. If there were someone used to wrangling Wildings, it had to be the matriarch of the River pack. Owen hustled through the kitchen, waving hello to the familiar faces and heading out back. Sure enough, he found Jace with several shifters gathered around him, handing out instructions on the proper care of the stables. Owen had done plenty of ranching back home, but he'd much rather put his Army skills to use at Riverwise.

He expected to wait off to the side until Jace was done, but as soon as Jace caught sight of him, he waved off the others and gestured for Owen to walk with him.

As soon as they were out of hearing distance, heading for the mountains out the back of the River family estate, Jace spoke up. "How's it going at Wylderide? You guys have had a hell of a couple days."

Owen nodded, solemnly. "Nova's shook up bad and twice as stubborn now as she was to begin with."

Jace smirked. "That sounds familiar." They were passing the cabins at the end of the stables, and Piper waved from inside where she was hanging curtains.

Owen lifted his chin as they passed, then waited a moment more, so she wouldn't hear. "You married one of them," Owen said, quietly. "Is there ever any talking some sense into them?"

Jace gave him an appraising look. "I guess that depends on what kind of sense you're talking them into." He narrowed his eyes. "Did you finally manage to get her up here?"

"Only to pick up some of my stuff so I can stay over at her apartment keeping watch on her."

Both of Jace's eyebrows lifted. "How close of a watch are we keeping?"

Owen bit his lip and studied the dirt for a while. This was what he wanted to ask, but he wasn't quite sure how to do the asking.

Jace huffed a short laugh. "I see."

Owen's face heated. "I wasn't *trying* to... I didn't intend..." He shook his head. "It's complicated."

"Tell me about it." Jace smirked. "Let's just say, with a Wilding female involved, I'm not exactly surprised things happened that you didn't *intend.*"

"Yeah, well, now it's a right mess, and I'm not sure what to make of it. I'm no good as a mate, not anymore. And she's going to have to take one soon."

Jace frowned. "What the hell are you talking about, no good as a mate?"

Owen stopped their walk with a hand on Jace's shoulder. "I told you what happened in those cages. They did things to me, man. I don't even know what... I don't know what I *am* anymore. I haven't shifted since..." He winced and stared back at the dirt again. "Look, that's just not going to work. But every minute I'm around her, I just sink in deeper, you know what I mean?"

Jace's frown was pained. "I'm sorry, Owen. I didn't

realize… Look, I don't know what's going on with the two of you, but I know this—loving a Wilding female isn't easy, but it's the best damn thing you'll ever do. Even if it's just for a short while."

Owen nodded. "That's what I thought. But if you want to assign someone else as her bodyguard…"

Jace cocked an eyebrow. "Seriously? You'd be okay with that?"

Owen snorted. "Hell, no. But you're the boss man."

Jace put his hand on Owen's shoulder. "This boss man says, if she's calling to your wolf, you need to listen to that. And there's no one I'd rather have guarding our at-risk shifters than someone who actually gives a damn about that person. Just tell me your feelings aren't going to comprise doing your job."

"No, sir." Owen knew that much.

"Well, then, we don't have a problem, do we?" Something behind Owen's shoulder caught Jace's eye.

Owen twisted around. Daniel Wilding was jogging up to them. He was Piper's brother, and he'd been an instrumental part of putting his father, Colonel Astor Wilding, behind bars. Now that Owen knew where the Wilding family had come from, it made a bit more sense how the Colonel could be flat-evil, even when his offspring were decent folks.

"Hey, man," Daniel said to Owen. "I thought you were down in the city, watching over Wylderide."

"Just here for a change of clothes."

Daniel cocked an eyebrow at him, but let it go and turned to Jace. "All right, I think I've got Terra convinced to stay at the safehouse for a while. At least a week, then she's got a gallery showing for her art in the city. Do you think we can get some kind of detail to cover that, or should I be trying to strong-arm her out of the art show?"

"Has she seen the latest video?" Jace asked.

Daniel nodded. "She had a complete meltdown. I think that's what finally put her over the edge and got her up here."

Owen had couldn't help but be proud of Nova for holding it together in the face of that. Her stubbornness was making him crazy, but *damn* if that girl wasn't tough as nails. Which only made him want her more…. while, at the same time, making him want to kidnap her and force her to stay at the River estate where she would be safe.

He was such a mess with this.

"Have you guys had any luck tracking down this Wolf

Hunter?" Owen asked them both.

"Nothing yet," Jace answered with a tight press of his lips. "We're working it. The FBI's on it as well. Although, I swear, those guys don't seem to have half the tools we do at Riverwise for investigations of this sort." He shook his head in disgust. "Or they're just not taking it seriously. Hard to say. Most likely, shifters are still on their own with this. Per usual."

Owen expected as much. The hate group was outspoken about their fear and loathing when it came to shifters, but many in the human population felt the same way, they just didn't say so in polite company.

"Some things never change," Daniel added ruefully.

Jace nodded. "In the meantime, keep your guard up. Daniel, we should be able to handle covering the gallery opening. We've got more volunteer shifters coming in every day to help, and Jared's running some training exercises to get them up to speed on security protocols."

"I could use some of that back up for this tournament Nova is determined to attend." Owen still didn't like it, but he'd given up trying to talk her out of it.

"When is that?" Jace asked.

"In a couple days," Owen said. "I can give you some idea of manpower once I scout out the place."

"All right," Jace said. "We should be able to cover that, too—just let me know what you need."

"What we need is to have every Wilding up here at the safehouse," Owen grumbled.

Jace and Daniel just chuckled.

"If you can manage that, I'm putting you up for peacemaker of the year," Daniel said, then started jogging back to the house.

"Anything else you need?" Jace asked. He was throwing glances back to his cabin where his mate was no doubt waiting for him. Dinner was near, and the sun was starting to go down.

His time was up.

"No, I'm good." Owen left Jace to his mate and headed back to the main house. It wouldn't take any time to gather up his things—he hadn't collected up much in the way of possessions since he'd been liberated. He'd been living in a cage for a year; after that, a man's needs were pretty minimal.

But now he was basically moving in with Nova Wilding—and he had no idea how that could possibly work for any length of time. Either they'd drive each other insane... or they'd end up in bed together.

And his head told him neither was any good for his heart.

CHAPTER 8

Nova was inside a deep, dark cave filled with glittering, moving lights.

It was actually a small theater not far from Wylderide. The lights had been turned down for the exhibition tournament with only spotlights on the teams up front and rotating beams splashing across the audience splayed before them. It created a sense of dynamic motion, even though the teams were stationary in front of their oversized screens, competition-level mice, and high-end keyboards. Wylderide's sponsorship logo was stamped across the fronts of their jerseys, along with their team names—*BitShredders* and *ChillRoid*—and player names on the back.

A large screen over each team broadcast the gameplay, adding a futuristic touch to the rock-show like environment. *Domination: Afterpulse's* post-apocalyptic cityscape was overlaid with all the high-tech weaponry lists, stats for each player, their life and cash levels, and kill scores in the game. The crowd was remarkably reserved, but Nova saw more than one smartphone user snapping pictures of the not-yet-released gameplay map, as well as gamers scribbling notes. *BitShredders* and *ChillRoid* were the top players on the original version of *Domination,* and they'd all been given the new game ahead of time, so they'd have some decent strategies to put on display for the fans. With the release to the public in just a few days, the teams were here for the chance to show off, win some prize money, and take a shot at the trophy… and it looked like the audience was eating it up.

The tournament itself was going great—it was the tension between her and Owen that had her stiff-backed and off to the side of the stage. The past two days had been nothing but tension and glares each time he looked her way… or she looked his. She couldn't decide which of them was checking the other out more.

Right now, Owen was on the opposite side of the stage from her, directing security over his earbud and mic. He hadn't forgiven her for not hiding out in the mountains at the River pack estate, but that didn't stop him from watching over her 24/7, both at work and at her apartment, where he'd settled in with a small gym bag worth of belongings. Each of the last two nights, he'd escorted her home and silently taken the couch for his bed.

For the tournament, he'd brought in a couple dozen security personnel, both Riverwise and other shifters. Half were inside the building, scattered throughout the crowd, while the other half were outside in the streets. Owen had insisted on blocking off all the avenues surrounding the small theater and making sure each vehicle went through a security checkpoint with one of his guards before getting within a hundred feet of the place. She appreciated that he was so determined to keep her alive, even if he didn't agree with her decision to take the risk of coming here in the first place. He was being a professional, and that made things a little easier. She just wished he understood *why* she was doing it—that this was truly the launch of the new game, and the reaction of the fans here would make all the difference in sales when they released to the public in a few days. Her father actually being dead was the only thing that kept him from being here; she had to do the same, if only out of respect for him and what he'd built with Wylderide.

Brad had come as well, and right now he was up on stage, in between the two teams, giving an introduction to the new features of the game map that the teams knew about, but the audience did not. The casters would take over once the new round started, giving the play-by-play, but Brad was in charge of the warm-up.

He wrapped up his comments and headed toward her off stage. When he reached her side, he touched the small of her back as he leaned in to whisper. He'd been finding more and more excuses to touch her lately, and she caught Owen's glare drilling a hole into Brad's forehead.

"I think this is going great, don't you?" Brad asked over the music swelling to start the next round.

She nodded. "The fans are gobbling up the new game map."

Brad slid his hand up to squeeze her shoulder gently. "You look fantastic in that outfit. I have a feeling you've sold an extra ten thousand copies of the game just with *that.*" He ran his gaze over her costume, which was black and silver and represented one of the playable cybernetic characters in the new game.

She eased away from him, hoping he would get the message that ogling her at a tournament really wasn't cool. Then she looked for Owen across the span of the stage, but he'd disappeared. Her gaze flitted across the audience, and she found him again. He was working his way through the circuit that he made every ten minutes or so around the perimeter, checking in with the guards he had stationed at various entrances and exits. For as much time as she and Owen had spent together in the last two days, they'd barely exchanged a dozen words—but she'd watched him enough to learn every nuance of his body language. Today, he was ramrod straight in his posture, even as he bent his head to check in with one of the Riverwise pack members. Owen's narrow-eyed sweep across the audience was on high alert. She imagined he had a constant stream of curses going through his head aimed at her foolishness in coming here. Or maybe he'd forgotten about her altogether and was just focused on his work—but she didn't think so. Only a few seconds passed before his gaze found her again, zeroing in on her across the breadth of the entire theater.

Her face heated up at being caught watching him, so she looked back to Brad.

"We're almost there, Nova." Brad's gaze was intent on the screens where the gameplay had started for the final round.

"Honestly, I can't wait for it to be over."

He tore his gaze away and frowned at her. "Are you still worried about that video?"

How could she not be? She was having nightmares about it nearly every night. There was a terrible sense of waiting for the other shoe to fall, only she was waiting for a blade to come down on her neck instead. "I'm hoping once we get past the launch, that I'll somehow be less of a target. That probably doesn't make any sense, though."

"No, it makes sense. Wylderide is all over the tech news right now. Any crank who can't stand shifters might be taunted into doing something—which I don't think is actually going to happen, mind you. But if it were, now's a more likely time." He swept a hand out to the audience. "At least your bodyguard seems to finally be doing his job." Brad grimaced across the room, but thankfully, Owen was busy talking to one of the security guys.

"No thanks to you." Nova glared at Brad.

He looked taken aback. "What does that mean?"

"You need to stop trying to make Owen jealous." She narrowed her eyes at him, daring him to deny it.

He gave her a cool look. "I don't need to *try* to make the bodyguard jealous—I already have all the advantages. *I'm* going to remain at Wylderide. He's the one who has a temporary job. And I intend to send him packing just as soon as we're sure you're safe."

"That's not up to you," she said, hotly. "He's risking his life to look out for *me*. And just because I slept with him once doesn't mean you get to be a dick to him while he's around."

Brad held his hands open like he was completely innocent of all charges. "How am I being a dick?"

She couldn't believe it. Her face scrunched up. "Oh, I don't know, you're just touching me whenever Owen is looking and generally acting like a Neanderthal. You could dial back the *obvious* setting on that just a little."

Brad gave a small smirk. "Busted."

She huffed a small laugh, not entirely impressed, but at least he was admitting it.

He leaned in and brushed her hair back so he could whisper in her ear. "You're just so damn sexy, Nova, I can't help myself. And that costume is making me hot."

She rolled her eyes and shoved him away but not hard.

He gave her a devilish grin, but then his attention was drawn to the stage again. The round was almost done, and she would be up next. Brad lifted his chin to the casters who were just finishing their play-by-play of the final match, then he tilted his head for her to join him on stage. She took her time, stopping to shake hands with each of the teammates and thanking them for their participation. By the time she was done, Owen had returned to his station on the far side of the stage, his eyes glued to her. Nova took the trophy from Brad and held it up high. The audience roared their approval, and a chant went up for the winning team.

"ChillRoid! ChillRoid! ChillRoid!"

She handed the trophy off to the team leader, then made a bee-line for Owen, intent on telling him she was finished, and it was time to go. There would be lots of afterparty activities and milling around, but she definitely didn't need to be there for that—and the idea of being almost done, but not quite done, was creeping up her back and making her nervous. If something was going to happen, she had the twitchy feeling it would happen at the end, like it did at the VA hospital. Just as she reached Owen, Brad caught up to her from behind and tugged at her elbow, making her stop.

She turned a scowl on him, but he swung in fast and planted a kiss on her cheek.

Her mouth dropped open. He did *not* just kiss her in front of Owen. After what she just said! "Brad—"

"I know!" he said enthusiastically with a wide smirk, completely cutting her off. "This whole thing went fantastically well! Just like you said it would. You're an incredibly brave woman, Nova Wilding." Then he dropped another kiss on her cheek before she could wipe away her shock. After a quick squeeze of her arm, he turned away to talk to the *ChillRoid* team as they broke up and drifted across the stage.

Unbelievable. She was so mad she could spit. If they weren't in public, she would haul his ass off stage and tell him exactly what she thought of that little stunt. *Fucking Brad, marking his territory.* And then she might fire him, at least temporarily. Maybe *that* would get his attention.

As it was, she had Owen's icy, inscrutable face to contend with. "I have the car waiting for you outside," he said coolly. "It's already been cleared."

He didn't say anything more, just waited for her.

She was inarticulate with rage for a moment, then finally forced out, "Let's go, then."

Owen didn't say anything else, just led her out to her

waiting ride. They were using her car, but Owen was the driver now. She had an internal sigh of relief once they were through the checkpoints his security crew had set up. He waited until they were well past them before speaking again.

"So... Brad is your boyfriend now. Is he the one you're going to pick for your mate?"

She turned to him, eyes wide. "He is *not* my boyfriend!"

Owen dashed a quick look at her, then slowly looked forward again. "You sure he knows that? He sure was acting the part." He took a turn onto the highway.

"He was acting like an *asshole*. He's threatened by you, if you must know." She peered at him, but he wouldn't look at her. "He thinks you're going to steal me away."

Owen snorted, which was a weird, strangled kind of sound.

"Why is that *funny?*" The heat in Nova's face was ready to melt glass. She'd been having regular fantasies about Owen stealing her away—as if that were even a possibility—such that she had to keep reminding herself that it *wasn't*. They'd only had one hot sex session against the door. That didn't mean anything. And she *couldn't* run away with him, even if it was possible, because she had

Wylderide to think of. And yet… she had been so damn close to saying *yes* to that mountain retreat, it wasn't even funny. All these mixed-up, confused feelings had been churning inside her in a horrific powder keg, and his smirky little laugh threatened to blow it all up.

"Sorry," Owen said in a way that meant he wasn't sorry at all. "I just get a chuckle out of Brad thinking I could entice you away." He gave her a sidewise look, all humor gone. "I can't even get you to stop glaring at me, much less convince you to follow me up the mountains for a few days." It was a challenge, and she felt it—felt the rebuke of it—but at least he was talking to her again.

"Brad told me to kick you out of my apartment." She gave him a saucy look.

"Is that right?" He smirked, humor back in full force. "And yet, I'm still there."

"I told him to fuck off."

He outright laughed at that. "I'm sure he enjoyed that."

"He knows when to cut his losses and not push me too far." She eyed him to see if he would take her meaning.

"Well, then he's smarter than I am." Owen kept his eyes forward on the road and didn't say anything more.

The rest of the ride back to her apartment was quiet, but not quite as tense as before. They had cleared the air, at least a little, but then, as they were riding up the elevator to her apartment, Owen's mood seemed to grow darker. He parked her by the door of her apartment while he swept the rooms for lurking threats, like he did every time. But eventually, he let her come all the way in.

It was late—the tournament was held in the evening to catch all the after-work gamers—but it wasn't late enough to go to bed. They had dinner beforehand, so there wasn't even a meal to distract them. The last two nights, she had retreated to her bedroom, doing work in order to avoid his icy glare. But this time, she didn't want to.

If she was honest, she really wanted to drag him into her bedroom for some decidedly not work-related entertainment. But that seemed wrong, especially given he was risking his life every day to make sure she was protected. He was trapped with her 24/7 through no fault—or choice—of his own. Lusting after him seemed like taking advantage of his situation, somehow, which seemed a poor way to pay him back.

But he *did* seem hesitant to call it a night... like he had something on his mind.

"So…" she said, breaking the awkward silence that had fallen around them. "I'm still alive." She lifted her arms in victory.

He didn't even crack a smile as he shucked off his jacket and laid it over the back of the chair next to the couch. "Just because someone didn't take you out in the most public way possible, doesn't mean there aren't people still thinking about ways to do exactly that."

She frowned. "You could at least admit the tournament wasn't the threat you thought it might be."

He shook his head, not looking at her, and his fists curled up. She was making him mad again. He slowly turned and marched over to face her.

"*No*, I don't have to admit that." He would have been nose-to-nose with her, but he was a half-foot taller, so he was just staring down his nose at her instead. "I don't have to admit *anything* that might increase the risk to you. I don't want you getting any ideas in your head that somehow this was a low-risk event, just because you didn't die."

"You really don't get this at all, do you?" she said, her anger rising. "I'm not doing this because I'm stupid. I'm doing this for a reason! Brad at least understands what this means to me."

Owen's teeth clicked together. He forced his words between them. "Once this threat is over, I'll be out of your hair. And your boyfriend's."

"He's *not* my boyfriend!" She glared up at him.

"So you keep saying." He returned her glare. "Until the threat has passed, I'm going to do whatever is necessary to keep you safe. It's *my job*, Nova."

That part was a slap across the face. *His job*. That's all she was to him. With a casual fuck thrown in for fun... or maybe that was just part of the job, too. Keeping the client calm with a little mind-blowing sex.

She fought to keep back the tears. "You think I don't worry about all this? About dying? I'm having nightmares every night about that damn video! And the bomb that killed my father. And the grenade that almost blew me up. I think about those things *all the time*. But I know there are other shifters out there who've seen what's happened. They're watching me, just like this crazy-ass Wolf Hunter. I'm just trying to do the right thing—to not let this hate group win by scaring me off and killing my father's business by murdering him." She had to stop because it was getting hard to breathe. And if she kept talking, she really *was* going to cry in front of Owen, in spite of the bravado of her words.

"Nova—" He leaned closer, torment on his face.

But she didn't want his pity. Not a pity fuck or even a pity hug. She stepped back and wiped angrily at her eyes. "I'm fine! I'm just... tired. It's been a long day." She teetered, uncomfortable in her own apartment, invaded by a man who was keeping her alive, but driving her crazy in the process. Crazy with lust, crazy with anger, and just flat unhinged with everything that was happening.

Owen's hands stopped reaching for her, curling up instead.

She turned and stalked away from him, retreating into her bedroom where she could cry out her fear-laden tears by herself, where it was a whole lot less embarrassing. But once she had cast off her costume and angrily pulled on a nightshirt, the tears fled, leaving only emptiness behind. It was true that her nightmares were filled with visions of dismembered wolves and bloody butcher knives and explosions that tore her into pieces even before the Wolf Hunter could get his blades into her, but her dreams were entirely different. In her dreams, there was nothing in the world but her and her hot bodyguard, together in a fantasy world where that was all that mattered. She crawled into bed and burrowed under the covers, retreating into that dream-like state where Owen was whispering sweet things against her skin.

I know just what you need.

Dream Owen *did* know what she needed, even if the real one was angrily camped out on her couch, probably cursing her out in his head. She pushed that image aside and drifted off into a hazy half-sleep, comforted by the dream version of her bodyguard—the one that protected her, painted hot kisses across her body, and understood her heart all too well.

CHAPTER 9

Owen was in his beast form, thrashing in his cage. He knew this because he was too low to the ground to be human, but somehow his body, as it hurled itself wildly against the bars, wasn't visible to him. Or maybe he avoided looking at it. Or couldn't... maybe he had no control of his eyes or his mind as it was locked up by the fear and the primal rage wanting release... and revenge...

A thump woke him.

His heart was still beating wildly, his beast surging under his skin. He came fully awake in an instant, leaping up from the couch, casting the blanket aside, and lunging for his weapon, which was holstered on the table next to him. He froze, trying to contain the raging animal inside him. It had never been this close to the surface before, and that was freaking him straight out. But more importantly—someone was in Nova's apartment.

He waited, holding his breath and listening.

A soft clink sound, then nearly silent footsteps. In the kitchen.

He dashed toward the sound, rounding the corner from the living room to the tiny walled-off kitchen, flicking off the safety as he swung his gun around—

Fuck.

It was Nova.

She screamed in surprise and jumped. He checked his aim, yanking his gun up to point at the ceiling and reflexively pulling the safety back on. Something crashed.

"Jesus, Mary, and Joseph!" he exhaled out, all in one breath.

"Goddamn it." She was shaking head-to-toe, and in the wan moonlight falling through the one window in her living room, Owen could see the shattered remains of her glass of milk on the floor, a splatter pattern of whitish liquid and glass shards.

"Don't move!" he commanded, one hand palm out to stop her, the other reaching to lay his gun on the kitchen table a few feet away. "I don't want you cutting your feet all over the glass."

"I'm fine—" she said, lifting one of her tiny feet like she was going to step right on top of the mess.

"Dammit, I said don't move!" He reached out, grabbed her outstretched arms, and yanked her up and over the broken glass and into him. She was small and light, but the fast motion unbalanced him, and he staggered backward. Plus his head was still rushing from the dream, and once she was in his arms... his inner beast nearly surged up through his skin. It wanted her—*badly*—and the only way Owen could keep it under control was to give it what it wanted...

He pulled her small body up his bare chest until her face was level with his—then he kissed the hell out of her. One hand behind her head, crushing her lips to his, the other arm wrapped tight around her sweet bottom, holding her up. Her whole body responded to him— hands in his hair and clawing at his back, her legs lifting to wrap around his waist. Her head tipped up, and she opened her mouth to him. His need for her came out as a rumbling growl and an instant erection... but his beast, whatever it was, settled down, mollified by having her in his arms.

She was only wearing a thin t-shirt and panties, and the hot skin of her bottom was searing his hand… along with a need to have more of her. *All of her.* He was dizzy with the touch and scent of her. She was filling his mouth with her greedy tongue, and her hot core was pressed against his stomach. Her clawing fingers on his back said she wanted this as much as he did… but he wanted to make sure. And this time, he wanted her because she *chose* it… not because he'd yanked her into his arms when she was scared to death. *Again.* He wanted this to be more than just a soothing balm for her fears, a casual fuck to chase away the nightmares.

He kept devouring her mouth as he walked her clear of the glass mess on the floor. When they reached the door of her bedroom, it took everything he had to wrench his mouth away from hers and slowly ease her delicate feet to the floor.

They were both breathing hard, and her eyes were half-closed as if she was dreaming. The scent of her arousal was driving him mad, but he forced himself to release her body and just hold her cheeks with his fingertips.

"Nova..." God, there was so much ache in his voice. "What are you doing, sneaking around in the middle of the night? I almost—" He stopped. Because he hadn't really been in danger of shooting her—his reflexes were better than that. It was the shifting that he couldn't control. And he'd almost let loose the thing inside him, which was not only dangerous to *her,* it was possibly deadly to *him.*

She grimaced and pulled away from him, wrapping her arms around her chest, closing herself off to him again. "I'm sorry." She shivered—he couldn't tell if it was arousal or fear. Maybe both. "I had a nightmare, and I just... I didn't mean to wake you..." Her shaking got more intense, a full-body thing, and he couldn't stand it.

He closed the distance between them and wrapped his arms around her again. "I can think of better ways to wake up," he whispered into her hair. "But I can't say I'm sorry to have you in my arms."

Her face rubbed against his bare chest, and his erection couldn't have been more obvious if it had hung out a neon sign. God, he wanted her so badly.

"Take me to bed, Owen." Her lips burned the words across his chest, and there was absolutely no hope of him saying no.

"Yes, ma'am." He loosened his hold on her enough to hook his arm under her knees, then he lifted her and carried her into the bedroom. Her bare legs against his skin, the way she curled into his chest as he held her... this was stupid, he knew it. But even if it were just casual comfort for her, he couldn't resist. Because that was all he could have with Nova Wilding, anyway.

He set her down, then turned her away from him while still holding her close. Her hot, sweet rear-end was pressed against his erection, but she was facing the bed.

"What are you doing?" she asked, looking over her shoulder up at him as if she doubted his intentions. Although he couldn't see how.

He pulled her t-shirt to the side, off her shoulder, and bent his head to whisper against her skin. "I'm taking my time and enjoying this." This one time might be their last—and he wanted to draw it out. Her body shivered against him, making his cock even harder. He slid one hand under her shirt and roughly grabbed her breast, kneading it and pulling her tighter against him. His other hand held her shirt out of the way as he feasted on the sweet skin of her shoulder, biting his way up her neck. He wanted to sink his fangs into her, claim her as his own forever, but of course, that was impossible. His beast surged again with the thought, but he kept it contained by even more aggressively clamping his human teeth into her flesh. Her nipple was a tiny, erotic point digging into his palm, and her little mewling sounds were sabotaging his intent to go slow.

He leaned back enough to yank off her shirt, then dug his hands into her hair and pulled her head to the side, opening her neck to him. His biting kisses were wrenching panting breaths out of her, but when his other hand slid around to dive between her legs, she moaned so sweetly, his entire body clenched with need. She was already wet for him. His fingers worked her hot, sensitive sweetness, and that just ramped up her pleasure-filled sounds. When he slipped his fingers inside her, she arched back against him.

"God, Owen, please don't tease me."

He wanted to—God, he wanted to make her cry and beg—but his beast was ready to crawl out and claim her. It needed *more*… and so did he. He spun her around and devoured her in a kiss. Then he trailed his tongue down the length of her body, tasting her as he shoved down his sleep pants along the way. When his tongue reached her panties, he clamped his teeth on them and peered up at her. She was gazing down at him with a lust-filled daze in her eyes, her dark hair spilling down her chest. Her breasts peeked out, nipples hard, her chest heaving with her labored breath. She wanted pleasure from him, and he would definitely deliver on that... but he couldn't help wishing there was more than lust in her eyes.

He would have to take what he could get.

Owen released his bite-hold on her panties. "Have a seat, Ms. Wilding." Before she could respond, he grasped hold of her panties in both hands. She gasped as he ripped the sheer fabric from her body. Then he took hold of her hips and planted her on the bed, spreading her legs and kneeling between them. He dove in, tongue first, as he pushed her to lay back, one hand on her breast, the other lifting her knee over his shoulder. She moaned, and her hands went to his head, guiding him and pulling him deeper into her sex. He didn't need any encouragement other than the squirming of her body under the flick of his tongue. He loved the tightness of her rock-hard nipple under his fingers, but he had to release her to slide his hand down and thrust his fingers into her sweet hotness. She cried out his name, and his cock bobbed against the bed's blankets hanging off the edge. Her body tensed, already rushing to her climax. He kept working her until she got there, panting and clutching the blankets and moaning out his name. She shuddered her release, and his mouth ached to be on hers again. To be buried inside her. This idea of taking it slow was a masochistic torment, one his inner beast wasn't tolerating.

He rose up and quickly entered her, slamming his cock in and sliding her further onto the bed with the force of it. She cried out with the suddenness, and *Holy Fuck,* she was tight. He remembered it from before, the first time, but being inside her again was a little like dying and waking up in heaven. He eased in and out, slowly, but with enough force each time to slide her a little further on the bed.

She arched up and complained, "God, Owen, you're killing me. No more slow."

"Slow is how I like it, darlin'." He was panting, but the truth was he wanted more. *Harder. Faster.* A screaming claiming that would be the best climax she'd ever had. But he couldn't give her that—couldn't be the mate who would give her the best sex of her life—so he had to settle for tormenting her. And he truly didn't want to go fast because then it would be over that much sooner.

He finally had her completely up on the bed, slowly entering her and pulling back, and the moans that were coming out of her were straight-up killing him. He leaned forward, buried deep inside her and kissed her full on the mouth. He stayed there, slowly pumping, but hovering over her beautiful face, scrunched tight with pleasure.

"Open your eyes," he commanded, his heated breaths reaching her across the short distance separating their faces.

Her lips were parted, telegraphing her pleasure, but it wasn't until she opened those beautiful, dark eyes and stared up at him that he was truly lost. He gazed deep into them, and she held his gaze, not wavering even as her body shuddered with each thrust he delivering.

"Look me in the eyes when I'm lovin' you," he said, his chest tight.

Her hand left his shoulder and traced a hot-fire set of lines across his cheek. He kept thrusting, but he'd almost lost track of his body—all that mattered were her fingers on his face, her eyes staring deeply into his, the look of hope in them, as if she was seeking something inside him. The slow movement of their bodies, connected and ramping up pleasure with each pulse, was nothing compared to the intimacy of that look.

Oh, God, he was in trouble.

He knew the difference between having sex and making love, and there was no question he was making love to Nova Wilding.

He swallowed, thickly. "Tell me you want me." The words were an ache striking through his chest.

"I want you." Her lips trembled as she said it.

He thrust harder. Her fingers twitched against his face.

"Tell me *how* you want me." His body was coiled tight, his climax building inside him like a thunderstorm gathering and threatening everything.

"I want you…" She licked her lips between pants. "I want you like this. Always."

Always. The word speared through him.

But he couldn't have her that way.

His body shuddered with held-back passion. He pulled back and slammed into her, hard and heart-breaking, because that wasn't what this could be between them. He'd already told her that. He could give her everything—his life, his body, his heart—but not *that*. Not *always*. Not a mating.

He rocketed up the pace, pounding into her. Her head tipped back, breaking that soul-crushing connection between them. She cried out his name, and it bounced off the walls of her bedroom. He had to finish this, stop it before it broke him completely… but even as their bodies moved together, pleasuring and rushing each of them toward release, he already knew it was too late.

He'd already fallen hard for Nova Wilding.

And that was a heartbreak there was no recovering from.

CHAPTER 10

"Owen!" Waves of pleasure washed through Nova, surging higher with every thrust of Owen's insanely hot body against, and inside, hers.

He was making love to her, furiously—her body was so wracked with pleasure, she couldn't tell if he was suddenly angry or just driven by the same lust-filled haze that had wrapped around her brain. He'd asked her how she wanted him to love her, but as soon as she'd said *always,* something seemed to unleash inside him.

Something that was pounding his gorgeous body into hers in a fit of passion. She couldn't complain—all she could do was hold on for the ride.

He growled into the crook of her neck, nipping small biting kisses that just tormented her—she wanted the real thing from him. A mating bite. A forever kiss. The thing she'd always dreamed of, that she knew would one day be hers, and yet… she had never pictured it with anyone else before. Never *wanted* it with a man the way she wanted it from him. Her wolf was practically begging for him, whimpering for more, craving Owen as her alpha.

Her alpha. She tried to pull back and look him in the eyes, like she had before, but he wouldn't face her. He just buried his cock in her while hiding his face in her hair.

"Oh, God, Nova, come for me," he panted in her ear, tension strung tight in his voice.

And she was close, so close, but the idea that he didn't want her, not in that way, was tearing her up inside…

He pulled back, finally looking her in the eyes again, but his were glazed, even as his cock still worked her body… then his hand dropped to the throbbing nub of her sex, right above where he was sliding in and out of her.

"I know just what you need," he whispered, a dead-sexy look of yearning on his face. He gripped her hip with one hand and used the other to shoot lightning strikes of pleasure through her. Then he angled so he could thrust even deeper inside her.

She shrieked as her orgasm rushed at her, a wave that crashed between her legs and reverberated throughout her body. She bucked against him, riding it, and he kept going… until a roar worked loose from him. He sunk deep, pulsing inside her, then collapsed down on top of her, panting against her shoulder. He stayed there, still coupled with her until he calmed a little, then he withdrew and slumped on the bed.

Her body felt empty without him. Her heart trembled with the need to know: did this mean something to him? Did he want her the way she wanted him? Or was this just another part of his job? Taking her to bed when she asked? Giving her mind-blowing orgasms when he thought she needed them?

Owen lay still on the bed next to her, staring at the ceiling. He wasn't touching her. Her heart clenched, afraid of the answers, but she had to ask. She rolled on her side and placed her hand flat on his still-heaving chest. He closed his eyes, like this caused him some kind of pain.

That almost stopped her.

But she was nothing if not stubborn. "I don't do this."

He frowned, eyes still closed, then he opened them and turned to face her. "Don't do what, darlin'?"

"Have sex with men." She held his gaze. "At least, not often."

His lips quirked at the corners. He brushed a stray hair away from her face. "You're damn good at it for being out of practice."

She smiled, and his smile in return warmed her soul. Made her brave. "Please tell me it means something to you, Owen. Because… it means something to me."

He frowned and edged up on his elbow to face her. Then he cupped her cheek. "You have no idea how much I like hearing that."

Her smile grew, although a little uncertainly. That wasn't quite an answer. "My life has always been clearly laid out for me. My destiny set. When I dated, which wasn't often, I only went out with men outside the pack, and mostly humans, at that. Because I knew it would never amount to anything… that I would be mating with someone from inside my father's pack when the time came. It would, by default, be someone he approved of and who could carry on the company… but the decision of which wolf would be solely up to me. I kept waiting for the choice to become clear. For some surge of interest from my wolf, like mates are supposed to have. Then I would *know* which wolf was my destined mate. But I never… I've never felt this way—the way I feel about you—about any of them. *Ever.*"

She was telling him her heart, but with every word, his expression just grew darker. She didn't understand it.

"Nova, I already told you…" His frown twisted into some kind of pained look. "I can't have a mate. It's not that I don't want to—*I can't.*" He dropped his gaze to the sheets between them, clenching and unclenching them in his fist. "Besides, any number of wolves in your pack would kill to have you. I'm sure there's one that your wolf will fall for, eventually." He looked up. "Although honestly, I want to punch Brad in the face every time he touches you. Do me a favor—if you're gonna pick him, wait until after I'm gone." He winced a little, like this was already causing him pain.

She forced him to look her in the eye. "Don't you see? That's what I'm telling you—I've *never* wanted Brad. I don't want him *now,* especially not since I've been with you. I just never realized before how it could be with someone, not until I met you. It was like being lost in a store full of lemons and wondering why you never thought they were sweet." She drew a finger across his cheek and then his lips.

He groaned, reached for her, and pulled her into a hot kiss. She gave herself over to it, and her heart soared. She wanted to make love to this man again and again, *always,* just like she said.

But he broke their kiss and pushed her back with another groan that sounded painful. "It doesn't matter what I want," he said, the pain seeping into his voice. "And it doesn't matter what you want, either. The fact is all those experiments left me damaged, Nova. *I can't shift.* Or at least, I shouldn't. I don't even think I'm a wolf anymore—I've been turned into something else. I don't know what, and I can't risk finding out. You weren't there, in the prison with the cages and the serums and the experiments. They did things to us that... I don't even know what they were. But they were creating monsters, some kind of hybrid shifter creatures, and I think they at least partially succeeded with me. I don't even *want* to know what I am. As far as I'm concerned, they killed my wolf, and I don't want to know what they created in its place."

Her heart was breaking as she listened to him spill all of it. "But there has to be a way—"

"There's not." His expression turned hard. "The shifters who were changed into something else… it was bad. Not only were their beasts damn ugly to look at— some kind of weird mixture of creatures—but shifting into that abomination was a one-time thing. They literally couldn't shift back because… well… they were a mess. If I take that risk, it'll probably be the last thing I do."

Her chest carved out, hurting for him. She just shook her head, not sure what to say. "I'm so sorry." She touched a hand to his face again.

He held her fingers trapped against his cheek, closing his eyes and leaning into her. "Nova, I swear to God, you're the best thing that's happened to me in a long time. And I want you more than life itself." He opened his eyes. "But the truth is I can't give you the things that even an asshole like Brad can. And if all we have together is a short time, then that's what it is. That's what it has to be. And when we're done, you can go on and have that destiny you've waited for your whole life."

She had no idea what to do with that. He was basically telling her this was just a fling—but not because he wanted it that way, only because he wouldn't deny her the things that would come with a mate. She sat there, staring at him, her heart breaking and uncertain at the same time.

He shook his head sadly. "Or maybe it's better if we just stop now." He moved away from her on the bed, and she reached out to grab at him, to stop him, without even thinking.

"No!" She tugged him back, and he didn't resist. The pain etched on his face made her want to love him all over again, just to wipe that expression away. "I don't know how we can make this work, not exactly, but there's one thing I know for sure—there's no way in hell you're sleeping on the couch."

A small smile bloomed on this face... then he gave a small chuckle and leaned into her, snuggling into the crook of her neck. "I can't make any guarantees about how much sleep you'll get if I stay."

Her body responded to his nearness instantly. She dug her hands into his hair and ran them along the hard muscles of his shoulders. "I think you know just what I need," she whispered.

He growled, and there was nothing humorous about it, just dead-on sexiness. His hands skimmed over her, and his mouth nipped at her flesh. She couldn't believe the surge of happiness that caused her. Her wolf yipped, ready for whatever loving he had to give. She could love this man for a hundred years and never have enough.

And then it came to her in a sudden flash of clarity. Even without mating, even without submission, with absolutely no magical bond of any kind tying her to him, just the ordinary love that a man and a woman could share, this thing she had with Owen... it was already the best and most powerful and most thrilling thing she had ever experienced. If this was all that Owen Harding could offer her, it already beat the hell out everything she'd ever had before.

She didn't care about mating, not at that moment—not ever, if it meant giving him up. But being with Owen would cost more than just having a mate. How could she choose between her own happiness and her father's company? *Her* company. How could she let it all fall apart just because she was falling in love with the wrong man? The stubborn part inside her refused to believe there wasn't a solution to this problem... but she couldn't see it, not at this moment with Owen's hands caressing her breasts and moving lower, wrenching pleasure out of her.

She just needed a little more time.

Once the beta was released, once the threat of the hate group was gone, once Owen wasn't trapped living with her… then they could figure out how to solve this problem. And if Owen still wanted her then, she would give up on having a mate. She would give up having pups, too, because that was part of it—there would be no magical bond between them to make their pups strong. In fact, she couldn't have children with him at all, not if he was genetically manipulated the way he was saying. But she would give all that up to be with him, if they could just find a way to keep Wylderide afloat. When this was all over, she was determined to find a way to have both—the man she loved and the company that was her father's legacy.

Filled with that hope, she gave herself over to Owen and his increasingly urgent attentions. There was a way out of this, she just knew it.

All she needed was a little more time to figure it out.

The next morning Nova was exhausted… and had never been happier in her life.

She and Owen were stumbling in late to the office. They'd showered the endless sex off their bodies and dressed like they normally would—him in a dress shirt and jacket, her in one of the costumes from *AfterPulse*— and they vowed to act completely normal. Not at all like

Owen had given her more orgasms in one night than she'd had in the last year.

But the glow must have been evident on her face, judging by the copious amounts of whispering happening behind cupped hands—and she wasn't even halfway across the office. When she and Owen reached her office door, she cringed.

Brad was waiting for her. "Sleep in late?" he asked stiffly. Then he narrowed his eyes, flicked a look from her to Owen, and started grinding his teeth, if the way his jaw muscles were working was any indication.

"We don't exactly punch a clock around here." She let the annoyance drip from her voice, but when she glanced back at Owen, she felt the blood drain from her face. His look of smug satisfaction was unmistakable. If she didn't already *know* they'd spent the whole night in bed together, that look alone blared it out to everyone in the office. Her tight-lipped disapproval only made him smirk more... but it was really all for Brad.

She turned back to him.

"Well." Brad's voice could freeze a waterfall in place. "While you were enjoying time in your bed, the rest of us were working hard to make sure the beta will be ready for release in two days."

She scowled at him. *"AfterPulse* has been tested endlessly. It's ready to ship now."

He arched one brow. "If you'd been in this morning, you'd know that's not exactly true. We've found a glitch that aborts gameplay halfway through when playing a certain combination of players."

"What?" She leaned back. "How is that possible? We've tested—"

Brad coolly held out his hands. "I'm just the messenger. The lead development team's been brainstorming workarounds. They want to meet with you in the design room." He sent a chilly look to Owen, who had already taken his normal seat outside her office. "That is, if you're ready to get back to work."

Something was completely off about this. Either Brad was sabotaging the launch intentionally, or they'd somehow missed a major operational failure mode. One that really shouldn't happen.

"Of course I'm ready to work," she snapped at him. "I'm here, aren't I?"

Brad swept his hand out, gesturing down the hall toward the design room—it was a war room of sorts where they gathered with the coders to brainstorm solutions to unexpected gameplay problems.

Owen rose up to follow.

Brad glared at him. "It's the *design* room. I think she'll be safe."

The last thing she wanted was Owen's presence in the middle of a design review—those sessions were heated as it was, and she could tell the two of them were ready to brawl at the slightest provocation.

She waved Owen back into his seat. "I'll check back when I'm done." She gave Brad a pinched look. "I doubt this is anything serious. I won't be long."

He just tipped his head for her to go first.

Nova marched toward the design room, leaving a fairly pissed-off looking Owen behind. She'd have to figure out a way to keep them from killing each other while she sorted out this newfound relationship with Owen—for now, she would just have to keep them apart.

When she and Brad reached the design room, the lights were off. She strode in and waved her hand at the motion-activated controls, looking around at the empty room in confusion. Brad followed her in and closed the door behind him.

What the hell? "So… I take it there's actually *not* a problem with the game." She crossed her arms over her chest. "What's this really about?"

His lips pressed into a straight line as he covered the distance between them in three long strides. He loomed over her.

"You're losing your way, Nova." His voice had a hard edge to it.

"What the hell are you talking about?" A flutter of panic rose up in her throat. Brad would never hurt her, but something was up... and she didn't like it.

"You're distracted. It's not just your father's death. Or the attack. It's this bodyguard... he's no good for you."

Her face flamed. "I've already told you, that's none of your business."

His hard expression didn't change. "Oh, but it is. And you know it. What's more, the rest of the pack knows it, too."

Her heart fluttered again. *The rest of the pack?* "What do you mean?"

Brad stepped closer. "They've seen the way you look at him. The way you've brought him into your apartment. It doesn't take a genius to figure out you two are fucking each other's brains out—"

"Fuck you!" She jabbed a finger at him. "You don't get to tell me—"

"*No,*" he cut her off, his dark eyes glittering. "I don't

get to tell you how to run your life. But I told you already—the pack won't wait forever for you to pick a mate. And now that it looks like you have… only he's not one of us…"

Her eyes went wide. "What are you saying?"

He nodded, knowingly. "There's talk—lots of talk— of leaving Wylderide. Lead developers, head coders, all the key players. They're talking about taking the game engine with them and rebuilding on their own."

"What? They can't… they wouldn't…" She was sputtering with disbelief. "You have to stop them!"

"With what, exactly?" His expression grew harsh. "Promises that you'll pick one of them eventually? Or me? They've seen us fighting, Nova. And to be honest… there's not much reason for me to stay, either."

Her mouth ran dry. Everything was falling apart. If Brad took the lead staff… they'd never get the game out the door. And even if they did, there would be no support. Wylderide would implode, collapsing due to a talent drain from within.

"Brad… no…" Tears had jumped to her eyes. *Ruined.* All of it, ruined. She couldn't hold her father's company together for even a month after his death.

She had failed him. *Completely.*

Brad edged closer, his expression softening. "I know. I don't want this to happen, Nova, I swear. I've tried to talk them out of it, but the only way they'll stay is if…"

She blinked back the tears and peered up at him. "What? What is it?"

He grimaced. "They're looking to me as their alpha. It's what the pack wants. You know that's how it works—they need a leader, and they've already decided I'm it. If you're off with someone else…"

Her mouth fell open. It was getting hard for her to breathe. "They'd turn to you anyway." And now that she knew Owen couldn't shift, it was clear he could never be their alpha, regardless. If they would even accept him… which they wouldn't. Her father's pack would follow Brad. The company would go on, but it would be without *her*. And without her influence, her guidance, she knew exactly what Brad would do—he would port the game to consoles, add in-game purchases, all the things her father would never have wanted. The things *she* didn't want.

Her father's dreams would be a smoking pile of ruins.

Her heart was crushing under a tremendous weight. It hurt so badly she actually pressed a hand to her chest to stop the pain.

Brad's hands were suddenly on her shoulders. "It

doesn't have to be this way, Nova."

She blinked up at him, not understanding. "They're abandoning me. Betraying my father. He's barely cold in his grave—"

"They aren't doing anything. *You* are." His expression turned hard momentarily, then softened again. "It's not too late to stop this." He drew even closer. *"You* can stop this from happening."

She shook her head, a strange buzzing in it short-circuiting all her thoughts.

She'd failed her father.

"How can I—"

"You know how," he cut her off.

She stared up at him.

"Submit to me. Show them you've chosen me for your alpha. They'll stay. It's what they want to do, anyway. Do the right thing, Nova, and keep your father's company together."

"Submit to you." She said the words in a daze, and they were even more thick and awkward in her mind than they were on her tongue.

He ran his hands up and down her arms and drew her against his hard body.

She numbly didn't resist.

He pressed his lips to her hair. "You know I love you. You know I'll treat you well, care for you, just as your father always has. I'll carry on the company just as he would, I promise. We'll do everything in his name, to honor him, just as you want it to be." He pulled back and looked into her eyes. "But you have to show them, *now,* that you've accepted me as your alpha."

"Now?" A tremor was running through her. He meant *right now.*

"They're ready to bolt," he said, softly, frowning with concern. "If you want to make the release date—"

"I have to submit to you. To show them." A ringing in her ears numbed her… no, that sound was her wolf howling in the distance, protesting this. But she had no choice. She knew that. It was all coming apart at the seams, and she had to stop it now… or there wouldn't be another chance.

She'd run out of time.

"Submit to me, Nova, and this will all work out for the best. I promise."

She nodded, numbly, and then squeezed her eyes closed. She had to drag her wolf out of the simpering, whining ball she had curled up into, but eventually, she managed to shift. When she opened her eyes, Brad was already in wolf form, standing before her with his ears up, tail erect—the alpha pose.

Submit to me, he commanded, sending his thoughts washing over her.

A whine and a whimper came out of her wolfish mouth, but she stretched her front paws forward, raised her rump in the air, dropped her tail... and last of all, bent her head in submission. The magic pulsed between them, her submission bolstering Brad's magic and bonding her to him. It was just a temporary bond—until the next full moon—but it was strong. He was a powerful alpha, and submitting to him flushed her full of magical uplift as well.

Rise, my love, he said, and the words jerked her up from her submission pose and beat against her heart, bruising it. She didn't love him. Would never love him. But he was now her alpha, and any command he gave her, she would be hard-pressed to resist. Not without extreme duress for her wolf and herself. And soon... he would claim her for a mate. He would take her with his body and his bite, and then she would be magically bound to him forever.

This was her fate.

She'd thought she'd dodged it—thought she'd found a way out of it—but she was wrong.

Shift for me, my love, her alpha commanded. When she did, she stood naked before him in her human form. His tall, broadly-muscled body towered over her, his erection large and sticking out from his body. He swept her into his arms, pressing his naked flesh to hers, his hands touching her all over.

"I can't wait to make you mine, Nova Wilding," he panted into her ear, his voice hoarse, his erection pressing into her side.

She didn't answer. The shudder that ran through her wasn't pleasure… it was a numb sort of horror.

"Soon, my love, very soon." Then he planted a wet, possessive kiss against her neck.

She shuddered again and kept her eyes downcast.

He released her. "Get dressed," he commanded, and she did.

When she was done, back in the costume she had worn into work this morning, mere minutes and a lifetime ago, she stood before him, blinking and still in a daze. It wasn't just the magical bond and the overwhelming sense of connection to Brad—*her alpha*—that put her in that state. It was the inescapable fact that she had submitted to him, that she would let him claim her, and that the fantasy she had last night about belonging to Owen in any way had blown away like so much smoke from a distant, lovely fire that was now dead.

"You know what you need to do," Brad said to her, peering down to catch her vacant gaze.

She nodded and followed him out of the design room, down the hall, and to the chair outside her office to where Owen sat.

"You're fired," she said to him.

Then she turned and walked into her office and closed the door behind her.

Chapter 11

Owen couldn't believe it—Nova had just fired him.

He stood there for a moment, staring blankly at her closed office door. His brain was still trying to make sense of it, but when he saw Brad's big smirking face next to her door, it all fell into place.

"What did you do to her?" His body tensed up, ready to surge. His beast raged from his core like a volcano.

Brad crossed his arms over his chest, and his smirk grew into a small laugh. "I didn't do anything to her."

Owen lunged for him, unable to hold himself back

from wiping that goddamn smirk off his face, but Brad was more than ready for him—he met Owen with a fist to his face. It knocked Owen back, making him stumble. By the time he was ready to go again, a half dozen shifters had hopped the cubicle walls and surrounded him. Some had claws out, others just their fangs, but their snarls couldn't have been more clear. The only thing holding them back was Brad's upraised hand.

Shit. Whatever had just gone down with Nova—whatever she was thinking with this business of firing him—he couldn't do anything when he was vastly outnumbered by her pack.

Although… it appeared to actually be Brad's pack.

And then it dawned on him. "She submitted to you," Owen said, awe in his voice. He couldn't believe it—she'd been in his arms all night long, and then she strolled into the office and submitted to Brad? He must've threatened her in some way. And *that* surged up Owen's beast even more.

The smirk on Brad's face had grown into a wide smile. Owen's words—saying out loud that Nova had submitted to him—had rippled through the group. There were nods of approval and smiles of satisfaction.

"That was the plan along," Brad said, casually. "Or

didn't you know? You were always just a distraction, a little Southern trash to play around with for a while, until she was ready to get serious and run her business. She doesn't *need* you, Tex. Never did. So how about you *get the hell out.*"

His words were red hot pokers, stabbing through his chest with the truth—Owen had lost her. Never really had her in the first place. Whatever Brad had said to her in that conference room, she had submitted to him in a heartbeat. Now it was just a matter of time before he claimed her. For all Owen knew, Brad would stomp into her office, bend her over her desk, fuck her and claim her before his morning coffee.

And she had agreed to it.

Otherwise, she wouldn't have submitted to him in the first place.

Owen was speechless—and he could barely keep his beast from raging out. The tension in the crowd of wolves surrounding him clicked up a notch... fighting this was useless. She'd made her choice. If there were any hope of changing her mind, he certainly couldn't do it if he'd been shredded by Brad's pack. Owen slowly backed toward the door, keeping his eye on Brad and the others to see if they would attack anyway.

Brad just lifted his chin. "Tell Riverwise we're taking care of our own security now." A rumble of approval rippled through the crowd.

Owen made it to the door alive. But every step that took him farther away from Nova was like a dagger through his heart.

It had been four days since Nova Wilding broke his heart.

"All clear on the perimeter," a voice spoke over his earbud. It was Jace supervising the personnel around the exterior of the building.

"Copy that," Owen said into his mic. Since he'd coordinated the security for Nova's tournament, Riverwise had put him in charge of security at Terra Wilding's art exhibition as well. They had twice as many wolves at this event—half inside the gallery and half outside in the streets—partly because the exhibition was in the heart of downtown Seattle and open to the public, and partly because Terra Wilding was thoroughly freaked out about the possibility of being attacked.

It was a strange sensation, protecting someone who actually wanted to be protected.

Owen still couldn't believe Nova had simply

submitted to Brad of her own accord—she was just too damn stubborn for that. He sure as hell didn't believe that line of bullshit from Brad about her just wanting a fling. Unless everything she had said the night before was a complete and utter lie, Brad had forced her into this. The problem was, Owen couldn't figure out *how*... or find a way to undo it. Or even ask her what happened. Brad kept her locked up in the office or her apartment around the clock, and she wasn't answering any of the dozen texts and phone messages he had left.

He wasn't ready to give up, but he was definitely stuck on what to do next.

One of Riverwise's guards wound through the crowd in the gallery, heading straight toward him. When he got closer, Owen recognized Noah Wilding decked out in the black body armor that outside security was wearing today. The uniforms were meant to be a show of force, and so far, it was working. There had been no chatter or any indications of trouble.

"Everything all right?" Owen asked with a small frown as Noah arrived at his side. "Aren't you supposed to be on the back lot?" Noah was Daniel Wilding's younger brother, and they were both military. Noah had just taken a medical discharge from the Army and come back from Afghanistan, and Daniel was active duty stationed in Seattle. Owen had tried to place all the military shifters on outside duty while the civilians manned the inside.

"Jace sent me in here," Noah said. "He wants to know if you're covering the after party."

Owen suspected the twenty-one-year-old was hoping he might get a shot at party duty. He hadn't been stateside for long, but Noah already had a rep for lovin' the ladies. "I thought Terra wasn't doing the after party." Owen didn't see the point in taking more risks, and he thought she had agreed to that.

"No, sir. Apparently, things are going well enough that she thinks the party is in order."

Owen just shook his head. Wilding women were unpredictable and stubborn—that much he knew from Nova, and her cousin Terra was rumored to be twice as wild.

Owen cocked his head. "I reckon you'd like that duty."

"Yes, sir." He grinned. "There's a whole different breed of woman here. I could get used to this."

Owen smirked. Terra Wilding's black-and-white artistic photography of the city certainly did attract a different kind of female. Lots of black clothes and dark, soulful eyes. They were all human, of course. Female shifters were rare—and jewels like Nova Wilding even more so—which meant most male shifters found themselves in human beds more often than not.

Owen let his face go serious. "All right, I'll put you on party detail. But I have a question for you, first." He waited until Noah's excitement disappeared under his solemn stare.

"This isn't a question about women, is it?"

Owen shook his head. He and Noah had a lot in common, in spite of the fact that Noah was years younger than Owen's twenty-five. They had both been imprisoned, both experimented on. While Noah hadn't been in the cage as long as Owen, in some ways, his time there had to be worse—Noah's own father, Colonel Astor Wilding, had been in charge of the operation.

Owen held his gaze a moment. "I heard you went back overseas after you were liberated from the cages."

Noah's face took on a hard look. "Yes, sir."

"Why'd you come back?" The word at Riverwise was that Noah had returned to Seattle once he heard the hate group was targeting the Wilding pack. But he hadn't taken leave—he'd somehow swung a medical discharge.

Those could be anything from a fake sprained ankle to get rotated out sooner, often with the blessing of the CO for extenuating circumstances, to a serious PTSD-level meltdown that the Army wanted to make sure was on the records. For someone like Noah… a shifter who had been experimented on… it made Owen wonder.

Noah gave him a piercing look. "It wasn't as easy to leave behind the cages as I thought."

He nodded. He hadn't discussed this with anyone besides Jace and Nova, and he suspected it was the same with Noah—after all, how do you tell people you suspect you're a monster?

"Did something happen overseas?" It was a pretty damn personal question, and Noah looked as uncomfortable as Owen felt asking it.

Noah dropped his gaze to the floor. "Man, I'd really like to just enjoy the after party, you know?"

Owen put a hand on Noah's shoulder and squeezed briefly. "Sorry for probing, man. I'm just having some of my own troubles and… never mind. Not your problem."

Noah peered at him. "Permission to speak freely, sir?"

Owen smirked. Old habits die hard. "What's on your mind, private?"

Noah's young face opened, and suddenly, he looked

much wiser than his twenty-one years. "I was raised by a Wilding woman. I've got a sister who is an amazing person, but I sure as hell wouldn't want to cross her. Ever." He lifted his chin to Terra holding court with her fans next to one of her larger pieces. "And the crazy artist types are an even bigger handful. But I've heard the rumors about what happened with Nova. All I can say is that sometimes the Wilding women don't always make the best choices. But their hearts are always in the right place. Every time."

Owen pressed his lips together and had to fight back the surge of emotion ripping through him. "Problem is, I don't know if it's her choice or not."

Noah's face darkened. "If someone's forcing a Wilding female into something, especially with regards to mating... you do me a favor and let me know. My father was the kind who did that sort of thing. And I'd like to kill a fucker like that." He was dead serious about the killing part. And it was easy to picture the Colonel being that kind of asshole—the kind who would force a woman to mate.

Owen frowned. Had Brad forced her to submit? It was possible. But she sure didn't look under duress when she fired him. Sad, maybe. Or empty. Giving up. But she wasn't fighting it.

"I don't think she's been forced… not in that way, at least."

Noah nodded. "There aren't many men who could force a Wilding woman to do something she didn't want. Not without being mated first. But sometimes, my sister and our cousins get a little carried away and forget all their options. Sometimes they need someone else to point them out." He gave Owen a meaningful look. "Fight for her, man. It's what she would want."

Owen dipped his head and stared at the ground by his polished shoes. "Well, you know my life is really fucked up when I'm considering advice from a private."

When he looked up, Noah was grinning again.

"Go on." Owen waved him off. "Get back to your station. Tell Jace you're taking my spot at the after party. I have some business to take care of, anyway."

"Yes, sir." Noah smiled wide, then strode back through the gallery, weaving through the patrons and throwing a few flirtatious smiles to some of the younger women.

Owen just shook his head. But the kid was right—he could sit by and watch this whole thing roll out, or he could do something about it. If he wasn't already too late—if Nova hadn't already been claimed by Brad—then Owen was going to fight like hell for her.

CHAPTER 12

"I'm not sleeping on the couch tonight, Nova."

It was Brad—*her alpha*—leaning against the doorway of her bedroom, raking her body with his eyes. She had submitted to him, which meant if he ordered her to let him into her bed tonight, she would have to do it. Or, at least, it would be very difficult to say *no* to him. That didn't mean she had to enjoy it—any of it, even the sex that he so clearly wanted from her.

"All right," she said. "But the carpet really isn't that comfortable for sleeping on."

He glared at her, but she just turned her back on him. They had been having the same fight for the last four nights, although he did switch it up each night with some new attempt to get her to have sex with him. She knew him well enough to see the tactic behind it—if he could just break down her walls, get her hot and bothered, then she wouldn't resist when he tried to claim her. It was a great plan... except she had no desire to ever let Brad touch her. The idea *repulsed* her, even as her wolf felt the full extent of his attraction through the magical bond that tied them together.

And Brad was working that bond for all it was worth.

Nova dug into the refrigerator and pulled out a bottle of red wine she had been nursing for the last four days. Normally, she didn't drink much, but having that glass at the end of the day was about the only thing that kept her sane through Brad's attempts to get into her bed.

She poured herself a full-to-the-rim glass and raised it to him. "Cheers!" She downed half of it in one long series of gulps. The bitter taste stung her throat and fortified her.

Brad scowled and unlocked his arms, marching over to her. He took the glass from her hand and set it on the counter, then took her hands in his. "You can't avoid me forever, Nova."

"I must really suck at avoiding you," she said, "because you're here in my apartment every night."

He sighed. "I'm only here because I want to keep you safe."

Nova snorted. He was here for one reason, and one reason only—to claim her. She'd only ever wanted one man to claim her, and it wasn't Brad Hoffman. But Owen had to hate her by now, given the way she'd just fired his ass with no explanation whatsoever. But what could she possibly say? *Sorry, Owen, I've decided to sacrifice myself to keep father's pack together. Have a nice life.*

Tears pricked the back of her eyes, so she shoved that thought away.

Then she stared defiantly up into Brad's eyes. "I think I'm pretty safe here. Seriously, Brad, you don't need to keep watch over me and my apartment anymore. There haven't been any more videos released or any more threats from the hate group. They didn't even come after me at the tournament. I think they've totally forgotten about me. And we both know that's not why you're here, anyway, so let's not pretend, shall we?"

Just because he was her alpha, didn't mean she couldn't state the truth. And she was honestly glad that he hadn't commanded her to stay with him at his apartment. She would've been hard-pressed not to obey, and once she was inside his domain, his commands would be even more difficult to resist. It was like that at the office, since he'd pretty much taken over the pack, but he had the decency—or perhaps the shame—to not try to force her to have sex there. His apartment, on the other hand, would be an entirely different situation.

And he knew it. Which she guessed should count in his favor. But given he had forced her into this entire situation in the first place, she sure as hell wasn't feeling magnanimous toward him.

Brad's expression softened, and it speared a modicum of guilt through her. She knew he had genuine feelings for her... or at least sincere feelings about wanting to be alpha of her father's pack. It was hard to tell which. But that only meant the submission bond between them was stronger, based on real feelings, at least on his side... and more difficult to resist.

He lifted a hand to her cheek. She managed not to wrench her face away, but she eased back a little. He dropped his hand.

"I'm not leaving you to live here alone," he said, "not until I know for certain that you're safe. And you know how I feel about you—how I've felt all along. I want you to want this, too, Nova, even if you're fighting it. If I wanted to force this, we wouldn't be staying in your apartment... we would be staying in mine."

Even that much felt like a threat... like he was hanging that possibility over her head.

A surge of anger fought through the submission bond that wanted to keep her quiet, not talking back to her alpha. "If you think I'm going to be grateful that you're not forcing me to have sex with you—"

He tipped his head back and squeezed his eyes shut. "For God's sake, Nova—"

"That's what it is, and you know it!" She grabbed her glass of wine off the counter again and slugged some back.

His fists curled up. "I'm not going to force you to have sex with me. I'm not a rapist."

Finally, they were getting to the heart of it. "No? Well, that's reassuring. Makes me want to just fall all over myself in love with you." The wine was going to her head and making her snarky.

His dark eyes narrowed and took on a dangerous sheen. It ran a spike of fear through her, but only for a moment. She couldn't believe he would force her into anything. His pride would get in the way too much if nothing else. He wanted to *win* her, she could tell.

And there was no way she would let that happen.

Brad gave a snort of disgust, then ran his hands through his hair, but he backed off a couple steps. "We're meant to be together, Nova. Someday, you're going to figure out that being with me is *not* the worst thing in the world that could happen to you." He turned away, his shoulders thrown back with that pride she knew he carried around. "I'm going to take a shower," he called as he tromped into her bedroom. Her one bathroom was back there.

Nova's shoulders dropped, and some of the tension fled her body, now that he was out of the room. She sipped at her wine, but the trickling feeling of dread working through her body came straight from his words—because he was right. Someday, she would realize that he *wasn't* the worst thing that could happen to her. Right now, her mind was still filled with thoughts of Owen and how he had been the best thing that ever happened to her. Brad was just a pale reflection of what she could have with Owen, and the contrast was too stark. But eventually, her memories of Owen would fade. The actual possibility of being with him was probably gone already. There was only the illusion left, the dream. In reality, he must have given up on her by now.

Eventually, the overwhelming alpha-ness of Brad would break down her resistance. He wasn't a bad man, and there are many logical reasons why she should be with him. She just didn't think she could ever actually *love* him.

She finished off her wine and puttered around the apartment, straightening things that didn't need to be straightened, flipping through old magazines she never read. She was just waiting for Brad to get out of the shower, so she could claim the bedroom for her own, closing the door and shutting him out for the night. He seemed to be taking his time, probably working off his anger. She supposed she shouldn't rush that, anyway.

But when he finally emerged from her bedroom, it wasn't at all the way she expected. She was prepared for angry stares and harsh words. Instead, he stood before her wearing only a towel around his waist and a dead-sexy smile. His wet hair dripped small rivulets of water down his well-muscled chest. He held the towel closed with one hand, but it was clear that he was sporting an erection that even her heavy Egyptian cotton towels couldn't hide. His bare feet stood on her carpet, holding him in place, and there was such a raw, sexual energy rolling off him, it was hard to be unaffected. She didn't want him, but he was the kind of alpha any normal woman would be on her knees in a flash for.

When she finally dragged her eyes back up to his, the slow, lazy smile on his face flamed heat of embarrassment, and possibly guilt, throughout her body.

"Do you like what you see?" he asked with a smirk.

She dropped her gaze and shook her head. "Maybe you should get a job modeling if this coding gig doesn't work out for you." But then her face just heated more, as she realized she had just basically answered *yes* to his question.

He seemed to take that as an invitation and slowly sauntered across the room, until he was standing before her, half naked, entirely too close. His strong hand slipped around the back of her neck, and he pulled her close, dipping his head down like he was going to kiss her, but he stopped just short. She was pressed against the heat of his bare chest, the gentle massage of his fingers at the back of her head, and his heated breath brushing her lips.

"Kiss me, Nova." It wasn't quite a command, but the strength of the submission bond was overwhelming with him this close. Especially with him turned on—she could feel his erection through the towel pressed against her, which meant his desire for her couldn't be more plain if he had spoken it out loud. Which counted almost as a magic. "Please," he added, a whisper against her lips.

She shook her head *no,* but she couldn't pull away, and that small motion just ended up brushing her lips against his. He brushed them again, intentionally this time, and whispered, "I'll make it so good for you, Nova. All you have to do is let me in." Then he nipped at her lower lip with his teeth, gentle and erotic. His hands worked through her hair, and only when he tilted her head and finally planted his lips on hers, did she realize that the towel had dropped, and the full length of his naked body was pressed against her. The kiss was demanding and strong, and any other woman probably would've found it powerfully sexy, but she wasn't any other woman—her heart and her wolf already belonged to another man.

Kissing Brad only felt ten different types of wrong to her.

She pressed her hands to his bare chest and pushed back. "This your idea of not forcing me?" she asked bitterly.

A storm of anger gathered on his face, but it was

nothing like the hurricane that was gathering force inside of her. Here he was, standing naked before her, trying to seduce her with his kiss and the power of his alpha commands. But she felt nothing but revulsion.

"Call it what you want," she said, "you're trying to force me into loving you. That's just not how it works." She clenched her fists and tried to march past him toward her bedroom, but he moved to block her path, then grabbed her arms.

"I don't need your love, Nova," he said with an angry snarl. "I just need your body." And then he did force himself on her, yanking her against him and devouring her mouth with his. She struggled against him, but he just pulled her closer, his hands roaming across her body, his erection pulsing against her, all while his tongue plundered her mouth. Her anger was mute for a second, then her wolf surged up, shifting in his arms. She raked her claws down his chest, and he cursed as she wiggled out of his hold. She hadn't shifted completely, just enough to escape—she managed to take her clothes with her. She stumbled back from him and shifted completely human again.

"A true alpha doesn't need to force himself upon his mate," she spit at him. "You will *never* be a true alpha.

Not to me. Not to any woman."

His eyes glittered, dark and dangerous, and her wolf whispered, *run*. So she did.

She dashed straight for her front door and yanked it open. She heard him cursing behind her, and a glance back showed him fumbling for his towel.

She didn't slow down.

Nova needed to get far away from him—to breathe air that wasn't permeated by his magic, to clear her head, and to just get out before she decided to shift and try to kill him. Of course, she couldn't—he was her alpha—but that couldn't stop her from fighting back against him. Not yet, anyway; not until she was mated.

As she tore down the hallway of her apartment complex, she had the heart-stopping realization that he had every intention of moving her into his apartment. Because if he couldn't claim her here, that was the next logical step. He wasn't going to stop until he had her. She knew that now. And that sent tremors of terror through her.

She stabbed at the elevator buttons but abandoned them when the car didn't come straight away. She pounded down the ten flights to the basement garage where her car waited. It was past ten o'clock, and the parking lot was full with all the cars home for the night. She sprinted through the rows, picking up her pace and running as fast as she could. If she could just reach her car, she could make her escape.

Maybe the River pack at the safehouse would take her. She would just need sanctuary until the full moon came, and she would be released from her submission bond. She would lose her company—her father's company—but at this point, that no longer mattered. She couldn't let herself be taken by Brad. She couldn't be forever bound to a man who would force that on her. She would be living a nightmare of forced sex for the rest of her life. How she didn't see that before, she had no clue.

Tears were running down her face by the time she reached her car. She fumbled for her keys, panicked that she didn't have them, but then she jumped a foot when a huddled figure next to her car moved. She had to wipe away her tears before she could even see him clearly.

Tall, dressed in a hoodie, crouched next to her car.

"What the fuck are you doing?" she screamed, all of her anger at Brad ramping up and spilling out of her mouth.

The figure jerked up and whirled around to face her. She vaguely recognized him, but couldn't place the face.

His eyes went wide, and he unzipped his hoodie, reaching inside.

She gasped. *Run,* her wolf screamed. She whirled around and tried, but before she could get halfway down the row of cars, two sharp stings to her back made her convulse and stumble to the concrete floor of the garage.

Was she shot?

Her vision blurred, and suddenly, her limbs were horribly weak. Footsteps ran up behind her. She tried to crawl away, but a haze rushed her mind and took control of her limbs.

She fell face first into the concrete, and the blackness rushed in.

CHAPTER 13

Owen was so angry he could barely see straight.

When he heard Nova had been kidnapped, he dropped everything and ran straight to the nearest pack-owned vehicle at the safehouse. He didn't wait for any discussion, any plan-making by Jace and his brothers, or even to hear any of the details about how it went down. Because he already knew whose fault it was—*fucking Brad*—and he was ready to kill him.

Owen was lucky he didn't wreck the car during the screaming-fast drive between the safehouse and

Wylderide—the whole thing was a blur. All he could see was Nova in the hands of that mask-covered freak, the Wolf Hunter, with his butcher knives tearing her apart. If Owen didn't find her before that happened, Brad was going to die a very slow and very painful death.

Owen's beast surged against his skin, never closer to busting loose than it was right now. It took all his focus to keep that contained and keep moving. He punched the button on the elevator to take him up to the 24th floor and Wylderide's office. Nova supposedly had been snatched from her apartment, but Owen knew Brad would gather the pack here to plan their next steps. When the elevator doors opened, Owen stormed out, and sure enough, Brad and his pack filled the center of the open area cubicles. Brad looked up just in time to see Owen's fist flying into his face. He landed the punch with a satisfying crunch on Brad's nose and came away with blood smeared across his knuckles.

"How could you fucking *lose her?*" Owen's fury shook his entire body.

Brad shifted so fast, Owen almost didn't realize it before Brad's jaws were snapping at his neck. Owen jerked back and stumbled, but the momentum of Brad's attack carried them both to the ground. Brad's claws ripped gashes into his shirt and flesh. Owen clamped his human hands around Brad's muzzle to keep him from ripping out his throat. Then he rolled, trying to get some kind of advantage, but he was human against wolf, and those odds were not good. He pummeled Brad's face, going for the eyes and throat while holding his jaw open with the other hand. But Brad's claws were turning his chest into hamburger.

Fuck.

Owen screwed this up, storming in without a plan or a weapon. Brad's pack was holding back and letting them fight it out—but Owen was quickly losing.

He roared as another gash dug deep into his chest. He squeezed his human hand around Brad's thick, furry throat, but he could barely keep hold. Then Owen thought about Nova going under the Wolf Hunter's knife, and a deep rage welled up within him. *It was his beast.* He tried to control it, but he was losing that battle, too. Before his eyes, his fingers shifted around Brad's throat… only what they shifted into made him shudder. His hands had turned into claws straight out of a horror movie. They were a foot long, more like knives than bone, and ringed with white fur at the knuckles. Brad's eyes flew wide as the blades sunk into his neck—he stopped ripping into Owen's chest and started scrabbling at monstrous claws about to separate his head from his body.

Owen wanted to kill him, but if he let this transformation go any further, he might not survive it himself. Except he could barely fight through the red haze of his fury. Brad's pack growled around him, a swell rising up. Owen swiped at them with his free hand, flailing wildly while struggling not to decapitate Brad. The pack jumped back. He closed his eyes to fight the transformation, but there was too much rage inside him.

A metallic ding sounded in the distance.

"Owen! Oh my God…" *Jace.* He must've followed Owen from the safehouse, knowing exactly where he would go.

"Stand back! Everyone back!" *Noah.*

Owen stopped flailing at the wolves around him, but kept his eyes squeezed shut, still trying to rein in his beast. His hand of knives was still clamped around Brad's throat, but he was no longer in danger of killing him. Not that he didn't want to, but now wasn't the time.

"It's all right, Owen, you can do this. Focus." Noah's voice was calm.

Owen sucked in a shuddering breath and forced

himself to think of Nova—not under the Wolf Hunter's knife, but having her in his arms. He needed to stay alive for that, too.

A wash of calm sent his beast scuttling back inside him. The knives retracted into fingers. He opened his eyes and shoved off Brad. Owen shook like a ninety-year-old man with palsy... but he was in control of his body.

One of the Wylderide wolves helped Brad to stand. He clutched his bloody throat and kept his distance with a wary look. The entire pack had backed up, forming an open space around Owen. He'd never seen a group of wolves look scared like this—freaked out.

But Noah stood by his side, and Jace was next to him. They both had their guns out, but they were pointed at the floor. Owen had a feeling it wasn't the weapons that made the other wolves back away.

Noah gripped Owen's shoulder, hard. "You got it together, man?"

Owen gave him a shaky nod.

Jace stepped in front of Owen and faced the pack. "All right, listen up, assholes. This guy..." He pointed to Brad. "Is my least favorite shifter on the planet at the moment, but we're missing a girl, and we need to find her. So we're going to put all this the fuck behind us and focus on the mission at hand. Are we clear?"

There was an uneasy rumble through the pack. They looked to Brad for guidance. Of course... he was their alpha now.

Owen raised a hand to point at Brad, and a surge of satisfaction ran through him to see the man flinch. "You're going to tell us exactly what happened when you lost her. And you're going to let me clean up your fucking mess until we find her again."

Brad snarled, but he didn't say anything. Then he glanced at the pack, and even Owen could tell he was losing face. After all, Nova was snatched under his watch. When Owen was her bodyguard, she'd survived an attempt on her life.

Finally, Brad straightened and pulled his bloody hand away from his throat, looking at it with disgust. "Of course, we'll take any help Riverwise would like to give in finding Nova."

It seemed like a sigh of relief went through the pack. These people were programmers and coders and game designers—not fucking security. As their alpha, Brad shouldn't have been asking them to take on that role. He should have been looking out for all of them... including Nova.

"All right, then." Jace ran a look over Owen's shredded and bloody clothes. "You ready to get to work?"

The gashes on his chest hurt like hell, but they were already healing. Owen gave him a quick nod.

Jace pointed to Brad. "You going to live?"

Brad curled a lip. "How about you fuck off?"

"I'll take that as a *yes,*" Jace said. "The rest of you are a bunch of computer nerds, right? Nova's been kidnapped by a psycho somewhere in the city. We've already got Riverwise searching the city's public cameras for any trace of her. We could use some of your servers to crunch the data. I'll get our guys to call in, and you can hook that up."

There were a few murmurs and a lot of nods, but even Owen could see the hope lighting up their faces. He wished he could share it—he knew how long the odds of that kind of search were, and that the clock was ticking for Nova even as they spoke. He didn't want to let his mind go there, but a part of it already knew they would never find her, except in pieces. And then he would fucking kill Brad Hoffman.

The pack drifted back to their desks.

Noah tugged him away from the still glaring Brad and

spoke softly. "Hey, man, was that the first time you shifted? I mean, after the cages? Jace told me what you were thinking…" He left the rest unspoken. Too many ears to overhear.

Owen nodded. "You weren't in there as long as I was. You didn't see the things I saw. The monsters they were making."

Noah narrowed his eyes. "I may not have been there long, but trust me, I saw some pretty nasty shit. And they gave me all the latest serums."

Owen frowned, not sure what he meant by that.

"The question is," Noah said, "are you able to control it?"

Owen grimaced. "Yeah. Barely. Maybe."

Noah nodded. "The fact that you survived all that time… I'm thinking that means something."

Owen squinted at him. "I figured I was just lucky, outlasting everyone. Or unlucky, depending on how you look at it."

Noah's face went solemn. "Luck had nothing to do with any of it. Those bastards had everything planned out."

Owen nodded. He and Noah needed to talk—especially about what happened overseas, after his time in the cages. But before he could ask, a round of swearing went up on one side of cubicle land.

"Brad, come see this!" someone called.

Jace was on the phone talking to someone, probably Riverwise, but he shut it off. He, Owen, and Noah hurried over to where the entire pack was gathering around one screen.

A new video.

A wash of nausea flooded Owen. It was a video of Nova, trapped in a cage, with some psycho poking at her with a cattle prod. There was a large, red digital clock counting down in one corner. It took Owen a moment to figure out that it was live streaming, not a recording. A torrent of emotions ran through him—*she was alive!* But what the fuck was happening?

"What the hell is this?" That was Brad, who had finally fought through the pack to see the video.

On the screen, the man with the cattle prod laughed as she jerked back and screamed. A roaring growl simultaneously went up from every shifter in the room.

The man turned to face the camera, then stalked toward it. For a moment, his hoodie and metal-looking facemask filled the screen. He was making some kind of adjustment to the camera, and it shook. The mask was different than the last video. This time, it was more futuristic—almost like battle armor for a future soldier.

When the Wolf Hunter stepped back, the view had broadened to take in the whole area around Nova's cage. Black rectangular bricks were stacked around the cage, connected by wires. They looked suspiciously like explosives. Nova huddled in the corner, sobbing, and the sound was ripping out Owen's heart.

"Well, here we are folks!" The Wolf Hunter's voice was light and snappy. Sick fucking bastard. "We've got ourselves a real, live shifter. She might look like just a girl, but trust me, she's not. Let's see if we can get her to shift and show her true nature, shall we?"

He went back to the cage. The electric spark and Nova's scream filled the dead silence in the Wylderide office.

The Wolf Hunter laughed again and step back. "You'll notice that the bars aren't all that strong. If she shifts, she'll have enough strength to get out. If she doesn't, she'll be stuck inside until the bomb goes off." He gestured at the explosives ringed around the cage. "It's not all that pretty, but I assure you, there's more than enough to blow up a little she-wolf." His face loomed into the camera. "Of course, either way, I promise she'll be dead by the end of our livestream. At which point, I'll be demonstrating those dissection tips from my previous video. You can see the countdown in the corner. Make sure you share the link with all your friends! Time for them to see that this is all real. No tricks, no movie magic. This is one hundred percent shifter Red Room. Payback for what they've done. This one will pay, and then another one after that, and another… until all shifters understand they can't just take our jobs and our women and infiltrate our society without consequence." He grinned. "Stay tuned for the fun."

Owen's beast wanted to claw its way through the screen and take apart the Wolf Hunter one chunk at a time. Every shifter in the room had the same look of anger and horror on their faces. Owen couldn't help going after Brad again—only Noah and Jace being there, grabbing onto his arms, held him back from plowing into Brad's face.

Instead, Owen just snarled and threw words at him. "If she dies, I *will* kill you." Then he shook off their hold and turned to the rest of the pack. "Let's go find our girl."

The pack growled as one.

CHAPTER 14

Nova's teeth were chattering so hard, the clicking echoed around her cage.

The man who captured her was stalking around the room, muttering to himself. She'd watched him talking to his webcam perched on top of his screen—and she'd never been more terrified in her life. This guy was a raving lunatic, and he had devised this weird set up to torture her and blow her up in front of whoever was watching. A full-body shiver went through her that rattled her teeth again. This time, it was loud enough to grab the man's attention.

He swung back to her, marched up to her cage, and stopped just outside her reach. He had the cattle prod again, but he was leaning against it like a walking stick, not thrusting it through the cage bars at her. Still… she shrunk to the back, teeth clenched in anticipation of another attack. The shocks hurt like hell, but they didn't seem to be permanently damaging her. Her shifter body could take a lot, which freaked her out—that only meant he could dish out a lot of pain without actually killing her.

He gave her a smile full of teeth. "Well, little shifter girl, you're not so high and mighty now, are you?"

He seemed to be talking for the audience on the webcam. His face was covered with a futuristic mask, but she remembered what he looked like from before, when he snatched her from the parking garage. She was trying to figure out where she knew him from, and it was driving her crazy.

She'd been so foolish, running off like that, angry at Brad, trying to escape becoming his mate. She supposed that was a pretty damn horrible fate—being mated to someone you didn't love—but it beat the hell out of dying. She should've tried to work it out with him, rather than just running off to find Owen. She'd been an idiot.

Her only consolation was that this raving lunatic had been messing with her car. He'd obviously been planting a bomb, and if she hadn't interrupted him, she and Brad both would've been blown up in the morning—Brad had stopped looking for car bombs a few days after Owen left. Although, with all the explosives planted around her cage, it looked like blowing up was her destiny anyway.

She stared at her captor—she had a feeling there was a crazy grin under that mask as he mumbled to himself and fussed with something at a bench off camera.

What the hell was his deal? "This is all just a game to you, isn't it?" she asked. She hadn't spoken much since she woke up to the cattle prod sending thousands of volts through her body—mostly because she had been busy screaming. But he was holding off on the torture now, for some reason. The man raced over to the cage and banged his cattle prod against the bars. She jumped and lurched away.

"Yes, it's all a game," he hissed. "Only this time, *I'm* making the game map and the rules, not you and your kind."

He lunged through the bars, reaching her at the back with his five-foot-long cattle prod. She screamed and twitched and thrashed against the bars while he electrocuted her. It seemed to go on forever, but was probably only a couple seconds. When he stopped, she slumped against the bars again. She couldn't help the sounds that came out of her. *Fuck,* it hurt so much. She had to think a way out of this, but her brain was literally scrambled. For several minutes after each shock, she could barely get her tongue to work right, much less think straight.

The man stalked away from the cage, huffing in disgust. She assumed he was the Wolf Hunter—who else could he be? He had the mask and the crazy hate thing going on. But even her scrambled brain was starting to put the pieces together—the mask wasn't quite the same as the other videos. And she knew she recognized him from somewhere, but she just couldn't get her battered brain to figure out where.

After a few minutes, when she was able to get her mouth to work again, she shouted across the room at him, "What do you want from me?"

He was broadcasting this. Maybe she could work with that—not give him what he wanted, whatever that was. Maybe use that against him.

He hesitated a moment, staring at the workbench,

then finally stalking back toward her. He faced the camera and spread his arms wide. "Entertainment, of course!" He turned to her. "And you're the lucky girl who gets to pay for the sins of your fellow shifters."

"What sins?" The lack of a cattle prod in his hands made her a little more brave. "What have shifters ever done to you?"

He shuffled across the concrete floor. "What have they done?" He asked this as if it was the most ridiculous thing she could say. "They *exist*. They take our jobs. They seduce our women for their half-breed monsters." He walked back to the webcam, probably making his masked face loom for his audience. Nova didn't know what kind of sick fucks would watch this sort of thing, but she was sure they were out there—he was probably streaming this on a Dark Web feed, the kind of place people went to explore the ugly side of their humanity.

He spoke into the camera. "These shifters are breeding with us, polluting our DNA with their genes. Taking our jobs, ruining our lives, destroying what it means to be human. They're creating abominations just like themselves, and they're taking over everything that rightfully belongs to humans. They have to be stopped before they corrupt the entire gene pool! This shifter is not only getting what she deserves… this is a lesson for all you shifters out there who think you can take over and become the dominant species on our planet. My fellow humans, wake up! This is fucking evolution, man, and it's a battle to the death! It's either them or us. We can do this—we're way fucking smarter than they are, and tougher too—but we've got to fight! These shifters are just a bunch of filthy animals, and it's time for them all to get back in their cages."

His ranting was straight from the original video Nova had watched countless times. It was part of the manifesto of the Wolf Hunter. But she still didn't understand why she was being targeted personally.

Personally. That was it.

The fact that she recognized him, even a little bit, even if she didn't know from where… that had to mean something. There was some personal connection between her and this lunatic.

"Wait, wait, wait…" she said, dragging herself up to standing as much as she could in the short cage. She hunched over and clung to the front bars, sticking her hand through to point at him. When he turned back to her, she was pretty sure everyone on the livestream could see her.

ALISA WOODS

"I know who you are," she said loud enough for everyone watching to hear.

He stared hard at her for a second, then whipped back to slam his hand on the keyboard in front of the screen. The small red light on the webcam winked off—he had turned off the recording. She shuddered, praying that didn't mean he was about to kill her. Then he whipped around and rushed at her, stopping just out of arm's reach again. He flipped up his mask and stared at her with eyes that glittered with his insanity.

"Do you, Nova Wilding? Do you know who I am?" He was taunting her. "Or am I just another one of those humans you brushed aside?"

She frowned. What the hell was he talking about? For a brief second, she thought maybe he was one of the humans she'd dated... but no. There had only been a handful, and she would've recognized them.

"Sure I do," she lied. "What I don't understand, is why all this?" She gestured to the cage and the camera. "When did you lose your fucking mind?"

He bared his teeth and growled at her, then he slammed his hand against the bars of the cage. It still made her jump, even without the cattle prod.

"I'm not crazy!" he shouted in her face. "I just finally

figured out what was really going on. Why everything always went to shit. Life is a game that you shifters have stacked against humans. You're the overpowered characters in a game humans are supposed to win. But we're going to show you! The Wolf Hunter... he's going to stop all of you!"

We? And why was he talking about the Wolf Hunter in the third person? And overpowered characters? He was talking like a gamer. Did he play or... the light bulb went on.

"You're that guy," she said gesturing to him, eyes going wide. "The one who applied to work on the textures for *AfterPulse.*" She remembered him now—he applied for a job at Wylderide. She interviewed him. He seemed to know a hell of a lot about playing the game, and his resume was stacked with all kinds of degrees and experience, but when she looked into his references, they were vapor. It was all made up. She hadn't said anything when she sent the standard rejection letter, but she should've known... he was living in some kind of delusional world already.

He sneered at her. "Yeah, the one you refused to hire because I wasn't a shifter! I wasn't part of your little club! Well, your fucking club is going to be missing a member now, isn't it? And this is just the beginning! I'm not the only person who was ever denied a job because shifters are rigging the game. We see what you're doing, taking over everything, all the good companies. I used to think Wylderide was the most fucking awesome place in the world. I played every game, every beta, every demo, and what did I get? The door slammed in my face. That was before I knew you all were shifters. But it all makes sense now."

Oh shit. This *was* personal for him—he wasn't just crazy—and somehow that made the icy trickle of fear in her gut turn into a gushing waterfall. She wanted to say she didn't hire him because he was a nut job with no actual experience in coding, but she was smarter than that. She knew he was a powder keg ready to blow, just like the explosives around her.

"Your name is Tommy, right?" she asked, trying to keep her voice level. "I remember that now, from the application."

He squinted at her and pulled back, but didn't say anything.

"Yeah, I remember it." She shook her finger at him like she was just now putting it together. Her frazzled brain tried to spin up a good lie for him. "You know what, you're right, that was a mistake. We got your file mixed up with some other guy. We were supposed to have sent you an offer letter, but somebody deleted your file accidentally. One of my idiot shifters, I'm sure, probably in personnel. Probably was jealous of what you could do with the game and didn't want you on board. But you're just the kind of man we need for *AfterPulse*."

He stood a little straighter. "Damn straight."

Her pulse quickened. "Yeah, totally, that's amazingly clear to me now." She swallowed. "Let's just forget this whole thing. We really need someone like you working on getting all the kinks worked out of the beta of *AfterPulse*. Come in, and we'll get you started. Heck, you could start tomorrow."

He was nodding, and a small smile snuck onto his face. "I'm glad you're finally seeing the truth about that." Then he gave her an evil leer. "Too bad it's too late." He chuckled as he turned his back on her.

Shit. She'd laid it on too thick—he was crazy but not stupid.

He went back to the camera attached to his screen and tapped something into the keyboard. His body blocked the screen, so she couldn't see what he was doing. After a moment, he turned back to her and slowly strolled back to the cage.

"I've put the feed on a twenty second delay. If you say my name on camera, it'll be Game Over for you. I'll hit the kill switch, shut the livestream down, and set the timer to blow you up thirty seconds after I leave the room. So keep quiet. And fucking shift for our audience."

He flipped down his mask and turned his back on her again.

A sick horror crept through her—her time was very, very limited now. He tapped a few keys, and the camera's red light came on.

They were live.

"Sorry for that brief interruption, folks, but we're back again, and I promise you the show is just going to get better from here." He turned back to her and prowled up to the cage. He pointed a finger at her, but also turned so he was facing the camera. "You shifters are denying jobs to ordinary humans. You're taking over everything, shutting us out because we're human. Like we're not fucking good enough. But *you* are the animals, not *us*. And now the Wolf Hunter is going to take *all* of you down." He spread his arms wide again, embracing his audience.

The way he was talking about the Wolf Hunter—it

kept striking her as strange. Like maybe he was just a vigilante following the Wolf Hunter's instructions?

He turned back to her. "There's only one way this ends—you dying for our audience. But the longer you wait, the more pain there will be. Which works well for my audience and for me. It's time you shifters suffered for what you've done. But if you shift now, I promise I'll actually kill you before I dissect you." He gave a small smirk to the camera. He was lying completely about that.

"I'm not doing what you want, no matter what you say." She was saying it for the audience, too. Because if this was truly streaming, she prayed Brad would find it.

And come for her.

She had no idea how he would find her—she was in a barren basement, no windows, no clues. Her only hope was to hold out until he arrived.

Her torturer raised his hands again, maniacal glee on his face for the camera. "Oh, I was hoping you might say that, little wolf. You're not so big and bad after all, are you?"

He strolled over to the work bench and snatched up the cattle prod again.

Nova squeezed her eyes shut, and prayed Brad would get there soon.

Before her resolve gave out, and she let this madman kill her to end the pain.

CHAPTER 15

Owen was going mad trying to not look at the screen. Jace was watching the livestream of Nova's torture—almost no one else could bear it. Even he was making low growling sounds almost continuously. He wore headphones so he could hear what was happening without the rest of them—Owen, Noah, Brad, and Brad's pack—having to listen. But *someone* had to keep watch, partly to make sure Nova was still alive, and partly to scan the livestream image and sounds for clues as to the location of the torture chamber the psycho had constructed for her.

It was past midnight. Owen would've thought no one would be up to watch this kind of sick "entertainment," but apparently the thing already had thousands of views. Which he really couldn't think about *at all* without losing his mind. He had to *focus* if they were to have any hope of getting her out alive.

It was all he could do to keep his beast contained.

"Okay, I've got something here," Noah said, sitting at one of the Wylderide screens. He pointed to a series of images he pulled up on email. "Jaxson says they tracked down the security footage from Nova's apartment and isolated an image of a blue sedan leaving about the same time Nova was snatched. No other vehicles in or out in a twenty minute time span."

"Good." Owen nodded. "Plates?" He paced next to Noah's cubicle, unable to stand still. The pacing helped keep his beast from leaping out, too.

Noah squinted up at him. "Only a partial. Just a couple numbers."

Owen's fists were already curled up, so he shook them out and kept pacing. "Have Riverwise run it through their databases."

"On it," Noah said. "And Jared's already running his facial recognition thing on the driver. There's a pretty good view of his face."

That stopped Owen in his tracks. "You have a picture?"

Several of the wolves at desks around him looked up.

"Yeah." Noah tapped the keyboard and brought up a fuzzy security-cam image. Owen reached him in two quick strides and stared at the picture. It was black and white, and the face was washed out, but you could definitely make out the features.

"No mask," Owen whispered.

Noah nodded. "Right."

Owen clapped a hand hard on his shoulder. "Good work." Then something jogged his memory—something Nova said on the livestream. He'd been trying to block it out, but it came rushing back. "She said she knew him. Right before he cut her off." He hadn't been able to watch much of the livestream, but he caught that part before he had to temporarily leave the office to smack his face, splash it with water, and get his head in the game.

"That's right, she did," Noah said.

Owen straightened up and signaled the closest wolf— he was one of Brad's pack, but that's what he needed.

"Hey, you! Where's Brad?"

Brad's head popped up from another cubicle, where he was doing what they all were—trying to find Nova. "What do you want?" he snarled.

Owen ignored his attitude. He didn't give a fuck about Brad—all he cared about was saving Nova. "She said she knew him. And I've got a picture of his face. I need all your people over here, looking at it and seeing if you know this maniac."

Brad frowned, but then he sprinted over to Owen's station. "Better yet, I'll forward it to everyone. We can cross-check it with our personnel records as well."

Owen stepped aside and let Brad tap away at Noah's keyboard.

Agitation was breathing down Owen's neck as he waited. Everyone in Brad's pack went back to their screens, pulling up the email Brad had just sent them.

"Anyone?" Brad called out after a minute. There were a few rustlings, but mostly silence.

Fuck. "She said she knew him." Owen went back to pacing and running a hand through his hair. "Who could she possibly know that would be part of this hate group?"

"It doesn't make any sense." Brad was frowning.

Owen ignored him. *"It's all a game.* That's what she said."

Brad nodded. "And he said this time he was making the rules."

Owen froze. "He's a gamer."

"Stalker fan?" Noah guessed from his seat next to the screen. "Maybe someone who didn't like the fact that shifters were making his favorite game?"

Brad shook his head, not disagreeing, but like it didn't make sense. Which it didn't. "If so, there's no way we can track that. We have ISP addresses, gamer names, but no pictures. No faces to match."

Owen went back to pacing, wearing a short line in the carpet in front of Noah's cubicle. "A lunatic fan? But how would *she* know him? Where would she meet him? At a con? A charity event?" He ran both hands through his hair. "Fuck, this doesn't make sense. Why would Nova recognize some random anti-shifter psycho? No…" He shook his head. "He has to be connected to Wylderide somehow. More intimately. He shut down the livestream feed after she mentioned it. He doesn't want us to know who he is."

"He's still wearing the mask," Noah added. "He must think he's going to get away with this."

"Because if we knew who he was…" Owen pounded his fists slowly to his forehead. *Think, Owen.* He stopped and looked up. Both Noah and Brad were watching him. "If we knew who he was, he knows we could find him! You've got to have him on file *here,* somewhere, at Wylderide."

Brad scowled. "No one at Wylderide would do this."

"A mole? A spy? Come on, man! *Think,*" Owen growled.

Brad growled in return but dropped his gaze to stare at the floor. "We haven't brought on anyone new since the funeral…" He looked up, his eyes wide. "But someone from *before* that. Someone we didn't hire. Wylderide gets a ton of applicants. We turn away ninety percent… and we keep intake photos."

"Get on it," Owen growled.

Brad raised his voice. "Everyone, listen up! We need to search the applicant pool, split up the files, scan them fast. The psycho applied to Wylderide. *Move!* Nova's running out of time!" Brad charged out to the middle of the cubicles, directing everyone's efforts.

Owen sucked in a breath and squeezed his eyes shut—it was getting harder to contain his beast, not easier. The more he was reminded that Nova was being tortured *right now*, the harder it was for him to control.

"You going to make it?" Noah had appeared at his side.

"Yes," he ground out between his teeth.

A ping came from Noah's screen. He hurried back to it. "Jared's got a hit on that plate!" he shouted.

"Found him!" someone else said, three cubicles down.

Owen searched for Brad—he was bent over the man's screen. "That's him!" Brad called out. He looked back to Owen. "I've got an address on Fireside Lane. Name's Tommy Rachet. Applied and rejected."

Noah nodded furiously. "Jared says the car's registered to a guy on Fireside Lane, midtown Seattle."

Owen whipped his head back up to Brad. "That's our guy. *Let's go!*"

He was halfway to the elevator before the rest of them were out of their seats.

The Wylderide pack had a couple vans that could carry everyone at once, and they had quickly loaded up, but they didn't have weapons. Jace had brought three guns, enough for Owen, Noah, and Jace. Besides, the rest of the pack was too slow.

Owen tore through downtown Seattle, running lights

and swerving around what little nighttime traffic there was. He was driving Jace's car with Noah riding shotgun, and Jace in the back with a laptop and the livestream. He still had the headphones on, so Owen wouldn't have to hear Nova's intermittent screams.

Hold on, baby girl, I'm coming. He was barely keeping his beast inside, not to mention the sheer panic that was lighting through his veins, terrifying him that he'd be just moments too late.

"Tell me she's okay!" Owen shouted back to Jace so he would hear him over the headphones.

"She's okay," Jace said, overly loud. "Hurry," he added in a growl.

Owen stomped the accelerator.

"Turn left here!" Noah shouted, pointing to the light just up ahead.

Owen took the turn so fast they nearly tipped, but not quite. They skidded, but straightened quick enough, and he stomped the accelerator again.

"Fuck!" Jace cried out from the back.

Owen threw him a look. *"What?* Goddamn it, Jace!"

"Hurry, hurry, hurry," he said, eyes glued to the screen, teeth gritted.

No, no, no.

"Two more blocks!" Noah called out.

Owen gripped the steering wheel so hard he felt it bend under his hands.

"There!" Noah jabbed a finger toward one of the tiny row houses up ahead, just like all the others they were flying past. "The one with the porch light! I can see the number!"

Owen drove the car straight up onto the tiny lawn and slammed to a stop. He was out, gun forward, and hauling ass toward the house even before the car had fully stopped. He ran full-on into the door—it was locked, but the thing was old as dirt and cracked all to hell. He stepped back and kicked at it, once, twice. Jace and Noah arrived at the doorstep and both threw their shoulders into it—it gave way. Owen shoved past them, scanning the dimly lit house—it was filled with trash and ancient furnishings and smelled like… it smelled like blood and electrical fire. And death.

"No," he breathed out, barreling through the dimness until he found a door with a sliver of light leaking through. *The basement.* He grabbed the doorknob, ready to yank the door off the hinges—miraculously, it was unlocked. He threw it open, and with Jace and Noah on his heels, he leaped down the steps four at a time. He

tumbled at the bottom, rebounded off the wall, and flew around the corner to the open, concrete-lined room.

In the center, was Nova. In a cage. Slumped in the corner.

Dead.

He roared, and his beast tore loose.

He lunged for the fucker who had killed her, shifting on the way.

CHAPTER 16

Nova's world was one, big, hazy stupor.

Her brain was so fried from the repeated shocks with the cattle prod, she couldn't even resist anymore. Or talk back between the bouts of torture. All she could do was save her energy and hope the magic in her blood would keep her from dying. She stayed slumped against the cage bars at the back, curled up as if that would give her protection. Her torturer had slowed down a little. Or maybe she was just losing track of time.

Hard to tell.

She must have actually passed out because a roaring sound suddenly jerked her awake. Her vision was fuzzy, but through the narrowed slits of her eyes, she saw a white blur leaping past her cage. It was big and loud and furry. *Wolf,* her mind said, even as her brain tried to sort out what her eyes were seeing. It charged for Tommy the Tormentor on the far side of the room. He was scrambling for something on his workbench. Just before the giant white wolf reached him, Tommy laid hold of a gun, whipped around, and fired rapidly.

Three bangs in quick succession weren't enough to stop the wolf—it was already leaping for him. The man screamed, and then his screams were cut off abruptly. The wolf had him in its claws... only those claws were... they were a handful of daggers.

Nova stared in amazement as the wolf sliced Tommy to pieces. Her stomach heaved, but she fought it down. Her shaky hands managed to grab the bars of her cage and drag her body toward the front to get a better look. Her legs had stopped being able to hold her up a while ago.

Before she could get far, two more men raced past the cage. She had to blink several times before she could recognize them—one was her cousin Noah, the other a

River brother. Jace, the one who married her cousin, Piper. They both had guns out and pointed forward, but she was pretty sure they hadn't come to kill the white wolf.

They had come to rescue her.

The relief almost took her down, and she sagged against the bars again. The white wolf stood over Tommy's body, which now looked like a puppet that had been torn apart—all the pieces of it were sort of in the right place, but not attached to one another.

Her stomach heaved again, but that motivated her to get moving. Closer to the front. Let them know she was still alive.

Noah and Jace were fixated on the wolf. It teetered and turned toward them—that was when Nova could see the giant red splashes across its snow white fur, blood seeping out and staining it. Noah put his hands out to the wolf as if to keep it calm.

"You're okay, Owen," he said. "You got this."

Owen? The wolf gave a small nod, wearily and not quite evenly, as if it was about to fall over. Nova tried to speak—only a small peep came out. It was enough to grab Jace's attention.

"Holy shit, Nova!" Jace hurried to the cage. "Noah, I

need keys for this thing." Jace tested the door, rattling it and trying to force it open.

Noah cast his gaze all around the room, looking for keys. "I don't see anything." But he kept looking. As he passed the computer, he tapped rapidly on the keyboard. The camera's red light went out.

No more recording.

"Are you okay?" Jace asked her, bringing her blurry-eyed attention back to him. She nodded and tried to mumble something, but all that came out was a moan.

"Noah, *keys*. Now!" Jace rattled the bars of the cage even harder.

Behind him came the wolf—*Owen*—limping toward her and the cage and leaving a bloody trail behind. She gestured to him with a shaky hand, trying to get Jace's attention so Owen wouldn't try to move before they could help him. *She* wasn't going anywhere, but *he* could be dying, and he was dragging himself halfway across the floor.

Jace's eyes went wide. He stepped back as Owen approached. Owen's unsteady lumbering finally got him to the cage. He bumped his head against the bars, dipping down so that Nova could reach him. She stuck her hand out and dug her fingers into his fur.

She fought with her tongue until she could make it behave. "Rest," she managed to get out.

Owen eased back out of her reach and gazed at her with crystal blue eyes. In spite of the pained look and the blood smeared all over his white fur, he was the most magnificent wolf she had ever seen. He lifted his snout, waving her back, then he raised his front paws. She got a good look at the blades he had instead of claws and leaned away from the bars. With one fast swipe, his claws sliced right through them. It made a horrible sound of screeching metal, but with two more slashes, he had cut a door right through the side of the cage wall.

Then he stumbled back, fell hard on his haunches, and shifted back to human. His naked body fell over and smacked on the concrete floor.

"No!" The strangled sound surged out of her. She reached for him with shaking hands. Jace had to help her climb through the destroyed cage wall.

"It's okay," Jace said to her. "I'll stitch him up. He'll be fine. But we need to get him out of here, in case the police show up."

Noah hustled up to them with keys in his hands, which were obviously useless now. He threw them to the ground. "The rest of the pack should be here soon," he said.

Nova ignored them both and dropped to Owen's side. *"No, no, no."* The words wrenched out of her, and her vision was blurred again, but this time with tears. She wanted to hold him or touch him or somehow stop the bleeding, but her hands were shaking, and there was blood everywhere. Something was wrong. He was torn up more than simple bullets would do, even close range. She sobbed and ran a shaky hand along his hair.

His eyes were closed, and his face slack.

A rush of footsteps descended upon them. Nova looked up to see Brad leading the pack into the room. Brad's arms went around her and lifted her up from the floor. Jace and Noah bent down to pick up Owen, and several of the Wylderide pack members helped lift him.

"It's going to be okay," Jace said to Nova, giving Brad a dark look.

Nova didn't know what that was about, but she could barely stand, so she was forced to cling to Brad.

He dipped down to hook an arm under her legs and pick her up. "Let's get you out of here."

The relief of being carried, finally safe again in Brad's arms, was so intense that she just slumped against his chest, nodding and praying that Jace could sew up Owen and keep him from bleeding out.

The pack was remarkably quiet as they all rushed out of the house, fleeing before anyone could find them. It didn't seem right. After all, *she* was the victim here. Owen had been rescuing her. But a man had died, and they were shifters… it was all too easy to imagine that going badly for them. It was an unspoken knowledge—shifters always had to take care of their own. Relying on local law enforcement was something that ended up with dead wolves all too often. And jail was no place for a shifter.

During the ride in the pack's van, Brad kept trying to put his arms around her, but she couldn't stand it, so she pushed him away. She sat alone, arms wrapped tightly around herself, quivering from the after effects of the shocks and watching as Jace pulled bullet after bullet from Owen's body and sewed him up again. Once the bleeding stopped, and the blood cleaned from his chest, Nova just gaped at what she saw. There was a multitude of slashes—giant, deep, and deadly-looking in their own right. Nova was no fool—she knew where those had come from. Owen had been in a fight with a wolf, and it wasn't hard to figure out which one.

Nova stared hard at Brad and hoped the accusation was clear.

He ground his teeth, but finally dropped his gaze and moved to the front, next to the driver. The van was tearing through downtown in the dead of night… probably back to the office, since that was where they kept the vans. She kept watch over Owen as Jace stitched up his slashed chest. Owen moaned once or twice, but Noah held him down, and he never really awoke fully.

She was glad for that, hoping he wasn't in too much pain.

But her heart was breaking a little more with each passing minute that he didn't open his eyes.

CHAPTER 17

Pain drenched Owen's body, but that wasn't what woke him up.

It was the shouting.

"He can't be moved!"

"We've been moving him for the last half hour."

"Stop being an ass just because he reached the bad guy before you. "

Owen's head swam with pain and not a little dizziness, but he forced his eyes to creak open. He was lying on Nova's cot, the one she kept in her office for late nights and naps. The overhead lights were too bright for his sensitive eyes, and he was still seeing double, but he could just make out the people who were arguing—Brad, Jace, and Noah. Nova stood off to the side, and his gaze connected with hers—she had been watching him sleep. Or be passed out from loss of blood on account of being shot, more likely.

"He's awake." Nova hurried to kneel by his side. Her beautiful face blocked out the rest of them, and Owen was almost as grateful for that as he was for the soft fingers that trailed across his cheek.

He let out a sigh, and his body felt like it might actually survive. "Hey," he said, but then had to stop because his throat was too dry for speaking. He licked his parched lips.

"Shhhh," she said, pressing two fingers to his lips. That simple touch sent waves of pleasure running through his body, fighting off the pain. "Don't talk."

She lifted a paper cup of water to his lips, and he nearly choked on the cool liquid as it went down.

"See? He's awake." That was Brad's voice coming from behind her. "We should move him back to the safehouse now." His voice shifted to a command tone. "Nova, give the man some room." If Owen hadn't been so weak, he would've launched himself off the cot and used his fist to explain to Brad why he shouldn't boss Nova around. But that was stupid—he was her alpha now. Of course, he could exercise that command. But Owen could see the struggle flitting across her face, trying to resist Brad's command and stay by Owen's side. That torment held him back more than the obvious fact that he was no match for Brad in his current condition.

"Are you this much of an asshole *all* the time?" That was Noah, and Owen could hear the fight in his voice just waiting to come out.

"Like I said before, he can't be moved." Jace's voice was hard as a rock.

Owen didn't want them fighting a fight that was useless. He really should go—he wouldn't be able to stand watching Nova under Brad's thumb, anyway. For all Owen knew, she and Brad were already mates. Brad certainly had enough time to make that happen since Owen last saw her. And now that she was safe, alive, and back in her office, Owen's job here was done. The bad guy who had been hunting her was dead. Owen had made sure of that much before he passed out.

Nova remained by his side, in spite of Brad's command, but when Owen struggled to sit up, new worries flashed across her face.

"What are you doing?" she asked, aghast. "Jace just finished stitching you up. And your wounds…" Her gaze drifted down to his chest, something he would normally enjoy, given he didn't have a shirt on… except his chest was a battlefield of scars, long straight gashes from Brad's claws as well as sewed-tight holes from the Wolf Hunter's bullets.

Owen wasn't exactly at his most attractive.

Nova's eyes snapped back up to his. "You shouldn't be moving."

He loved hearing the concern in her voice, but he forced himself to wave her off with one hand while the other gripped the side of the cot to counter the wave of dizziness that washed over him.

"I'm good." The roughness of his voice made that pretty unconvincing, but if he could just get a little help from Noah and Jace, he was sure he could make it back to the car under his own power. Maybe.

Jace edged around Nova and stared hard at Owen. "I'm not letting this asshole kick you out." He gave a skeptical look to Nova that was none too kind. "And *you* could be a little more grateful."

"No," Owen barked out. He wouldn't let anyone think

Nova was at fault for how she was acting. "Jace, she's submitted to Brad. He's her alpha now." The words choked him, but they were necessary so that Jace and Noah would understand—she couldn't go against her alpha's wishes.

Jace looked disgusted by this, and Owen knew exactly how he felt. He struggled to push off the cot without tipping it or losing his own balance.

"Could use a hand here." Owen peered up at Jace for help.

Nova reached down to help him stand, but Jace just snarled. "Hell no. I'm not letting this happen." He turned to Brad. "I don't care if you're alpha around here, Owen is in *my* pack, and I say he needs more rest before he moves. You owe him that much. Now get the hell out."

Noah joined Jace in forming a blockade between Owen and Nova by the cot and Brad's hot glare. For a moment, it looked like they might fight, but then Brad backed down.

He peered past them at Nova, directing his command to her. "I'll give him a half an hour. Then I want him out of your office." Then Brad turned on his heel and strode out the door. Jace and Noah were close behind. As Noah closed the door, he gave Owen a nod. He was pretty sure they would hold Brad off for as long as Owen wanted.

Long enough for him to say goodbye.

As soon as they were gone, Nova's arms were around his neck. "Owen, *oh my God*... I was so scared you wouldn't wake up." She drew back and held his cheeks in both hands. "I'm sorry about Brad—it's so hard for me to... to resist him. You know how it is."

"I know. It's not your fault." Owen ran a hand along the silky hair at the edge of her beautiful face. He was glad to see his hand wasn't too shaky. Her lips were trembling, and her eyes were glassing, and all that was tearing into his heart.

He swallowed. "But I have to say, it's going to kill me to see you with him. Pretty much every time. I should probably keep away so I can keep that pain to a minimum."

She was shaking her head. "I don't want to be with Brad. I want to be with *you.*"

He could see how hard that was for her to say, how much she had to work to get the words out, no doubt fighting the submission bond. It wrenched his heart that she cared enough to fight it.

He let his fingertips trace a small line across her cheek. "Are you already his mate?" he whispered. Those words just about killed him to say out loud.

"No!" There was fury in her eyes. "He tried to make me... I resisted."

His beast surged up inside him. *"What?"* He closed his eyes briefly, focusing on keeping from shifting. He was regretting not slicing Brad to pieces when he had the chance. He kept control of his beast and opened his eyes. "If he tried to claim you by force, I'm sorry, Nova... I might have to kill him."

She shook her head vehemently. "No, no, it wasn't like that. He just... he was manipulating me. You know, using his alpha command. And other ways." Her cheeks pinked up.

So Brad tried to seduce her. And it didn't work.

Owen's shoulders sagged, and he almost laughed—both in relief that she wasn't mated and that Brad hadn't tried to force himself on her, at least in that way. "You have no idea how glad I am to hear that." Then he sobered and peered into her eyes. "But I don't get it. If you didn't want to be with him, why submit to him in the first place?"

She squared her shoulders. "He threatened to tear Wylderide apart. It was only after I submitted to him that I realized there were a lot worse things he could do."

ALISA WOODS

Owen nodded. Before he could say anything more, she leaned in to kiss him. Suddenly, he was lost in the soft feel of her lips. He moaned and tried to pull her closer, but she stopped the kiss and leaned away, concern on her face.

"Am I hurting you?" she asked, frowning.

Owen smiled. "Only because you stopped."

She kissed him again, but it was brief. When she pulled away, she said, resolutely, "I want you for my mate, Owen Harding."

A smile jumped to his face, but it couldn't decide whether to stay. "Nova, I want you more than I can even explain, but it's like I told you before... I really can't take a mate."

"But you shifted! I saw you. And I've been thinking about this all the way back—if you can shift, then you can mate. That's all there is to it."

Owen's face twisted up. "You *saw* what I am, Nova. I don't know what my beast is, but it's not a normal wolf. They turned me into something else."

Her smile didn't dim one bit. "No, you're no ordinary wolf. You're the kind of wolf who charges in and saves me from a horrible death. You're the kind of wolf who doesn't give up on me, even when I've submitted to another man. I don't know how much you saw or how much you know about your wolf form, but you're not a monster, Owen. You're a gorgeous white wolf with some admittedly kickass claws. Whatever they did to you, they made you into something *amazing*. And, to be honest, it doesn't surprise me in the least. I don't know who you were before the cages, but have no doubt you were amazing then, too."

Her words charged him with a kind of insane hope. That, and the fact that she was right—once he shifted all the way, he knew he was truly a wolf. A different kind of wolf, to be sure, but still a wolf. And once he gained control again, that wolf was part of him. He wouldn't lose control again, no matter how extreme the circumstances. He had killed the Wolf Hunter with these crazy blades that were now his claws, but he had done it with intention. He'd been conscious the entire time and in control, even though the rage of his wolf made the Wolf Hunter's death at least partially an act of vengeance. But the man in him had no problem with exacting vengeance for all the experiments that created his overpowered wolf in the first place.

He let himself touch her again, fingertips to cheek. "You've seen what I am, and you still want me?" he asked softly, barely daring to believe it.

"Yes." It had to be hard to say it while she was still tied to Brad, but all her stubbornness was in full bloom on her face.

He smiled, but then a thought crashed in to kill it. "Even if I can control it, even if I'm actually some kind of wolf, I still don't know what kind, not really. What about pups? I don't know what I would pass on to them."

She threw her arms around him. "If they're anything like their father, they're going to be something amazing and beautiful."

And with that, he finally let himself believe it might be possible. He let himself hold her, then he pulled her closer. Even that small motion made his body ache. He must've lost an insane amount of blood to feel this weak, but Jace was the best shifter medic he'd ever seen, at home or when they were serving in Afghanistan. Owen was sure he would survive at this point; it would just take some time to recover his strength. And the idea that he might have somehow, someway, won Nova for a mate... he could hardly believe this wasn't some kind of fever dream from his wounds.

She pulled back and gave him a serious look. "Can

you stand?"

He frowned but nodded. He had to lean on her for support, but he managed to rise up from the cot. "Do you want to get out of here?" he asked, sending her a questioning look for why they were on the move. He prayed she wasn't sending him away. That he hadn't misunderstood all this.

She smiled. "I'm thinking maybe I need to spend some time at the safehouse. But there's something I need to do first."

She helped him to the door, and when she opened it, there was an entire party of wolves outside. And not exactly a happy party. Jace and Noah were still holding off Brad—behind him, the rest of his pack had assembled. They didn't look hostile, but if a fight decided to break out, there was no way that Jace and Noah could hold them off.

Jace's face fell he saw the two of them hobbling out of Nova's office. It had only been a few minutes.

Before anyone could say anything in the awkward silence, Nova turned to Owen. "Shift for me, Owen Harding."

He frowned and leaned back. "Shift?" Why was she doing this?

She smiled at him in a way that was so full of love, there was no way he could say no to anything she asked. "Yes, shift. *Please.* I want everyone to see your white wolf."

He didn't understand it, but he trusted her. With his life and his heart. He gave her a short nod, then stepped back to teeter on his own for a moment before shifting. He was more stable on all fours, and it actually felt good to be in wolf form while he was healing. The magic surged through his blood, and he could even feel it rushing to the points that needed to repair themselves. He still had the long blade-like claws that were the signature of his new wolf, apparently, but this was the first time he had a moment to look at the rest of his body. His paws and front legs stretched before him, covered with a thick, shaggy white fur. It tufted around the blades. He looked like an Arctic wolf on steroids, nothing like his normal black fur and claws.

A gasp went up through the crowd, pulling his gaze forward.

Nova had shifted too.

He just stared as she dropped into the submission pose—tiny paws stretching forward, rump in the air, tail tucked. She held his gaze for a moment, then dropped her head to complete the submission. The magic of it surged through him like a lightning bolt, lifting him and bolstering him with new energy. The healing in his body accelerated—she was literally pumping new life into him with her submission bond. This caught him completely off guard, so it took a long moment of reveling in the magical connection between them before he realized... he was supposed to release her.

Rise, my love. The ritual words he never thought he would be able to say tripped from his mind to hers.

She leaped up from the submission pose and hurried forward to run her muzzle against his. For a moment, there was just the two of them, rubbing faces. Owen's heart soared to such heights that he didn't think he even had claim of it anymore. It belonged completely to her. And this was only the submission... if he was right, a claiming lay ahead for them, and that would be unimaginably better.

A roaring growl pulled him out of his intimate moment with Nova. The pack, not to mention Brad, were outraged, teeth bared, snarls all around. Even Jace and Noah had looks of shock on their faces. Nova shifted back to human and stood before them buck-naked and proud. That simple act subdued them—they dropped their gazes, trying to shield her nakedness by not staring at her.

"I have chosen Owen for my mate." She reached down and started pulling on her clothes, nodding to Owen to do the same. Owen quickly shifted back to human and tugged on his own. He was stronger now, healing at a faster rate due to her submission. His mind was still reeling from that fact.

Just as the grumbling started to rise up in pitch again, Brad surged forward. The look on his face was fit to kill, and he was aiming it straight at Owen. Jace and Noah blocked his way, but it was Nova's outstretched hand that stopped him without even touching him.

"I have pledged submission to *two* men," she said, not to Brad or Owen, but to the pack. "Only one of them wants to force me into being his mate." She drilled a hard look at Brad. The rest of the pack looked at him, too, and subdued again. "I'm not going to be manipulated into taking a mate not of my own choosing," she declared to them all. "That's not how we run things here at Wylderide. Owen risked his life for me, saved me multiple times, and even guarded me before he knew me, just because I needed it. That's the kind of alpha I want for our pack. That's the kind of man I want by my side, running my company. And I'm going to make this *my* company, not my father's. I loved him, but he's gone now… and it's up to *me* to make the decisions that will keep Wylderide moving forward. I've already chosen Owen for my mate. That decision is not up for debate. If you want to stay, stay. If you want to go, go. But anyone staying will be pledging their submission to Owen as alpha of our pack."

Jace and Noah's eyes had gone wide, and Owen could hardly believe the words that were coming from her mouth. In submitting to her, she had freed herself from Brad's domination—she was pledged to *two* alphas, and that allowed her to speak her true mind. And she was choosing *him*. And, in doing so, she was taking a stand, bravely telling her pack exactly where she stood. Owen had no idea why this surprised him—he'd known all along how brave and stubborn she was.

The fury on Brad's face was priceless. It was all Owen could do not to smirk. But this was Nova's moment, and he wouldn't do anything to diminish it.

Brad sputtered for words, then finally forced out, "I've worked here for *years*! You owe me more than this, Nova Wilding." But his bitterness seemed to turn the pack against him. Their faces opened in shock, then narrowed into glares. He turned to face them. "She's been promised to me. That's what Arthur wanted. You *know* this is true."

There was a lot of whispering, but no movement.

"It's not what *I* want." Nova's voice was strong.

He snarled at her, then turned back to the pack. "She's lost her senses. How do you think she's going to run this company with an Army grunt for an alpha? I'll tell you how—she'll run it right into the ground. I'm not sticking around while some interloper comes in and takes over Arthur Wilding's company. We don't need his wayward daughter. We can do this on our own. Who's with me?"

No one moved a muscle. It quickly became clear that he was on his own.

"Fine." He turned back to Nova. "Congratulations on destroying everything your father built!" Then he turned on his heel and marched out of the office.

Nova waited until he left before turning to those who had stayed, pride shining in her eyes. "Thank you," she said, her voice rich with unshed tears.

Brad was gone. Nova had chosen him. But the euphoria of the moment started to wear down, and a wave of dizziness washed over him. Even with the bolstering of the submission from Nova, he wasn't healed yet.

Nova noticed and frowned, coming to his side. "You need to rest."

He smiled and looped his arm around her shoulders to draw her close. "Rest isn't the thing I want most at the moment."

She grinned and pulled him down into a kiss.

Owen wasn't sure if everyone in her pack truly approved of him. Or whether Jace and Noah were still hovering around them. All he knew was that he was holding the women he loved in his arms, and he would never let her go.

CHAPTER 18

Nova watched as Owen slept.

They were back at the River pack's safehouse, up in the mountains, far from the craziness of the city and the dangerous whirlwind of the last two weeks. It amazed her that in the short span of days since she kissed Owen for the time that she could be here with him, in a cabin in the mountains, ready to have him claim her for the rest of her life.

She had never been so happy.

Owen made a soft rumbling sound and burrowed into the pillow, but he didn't wake up. He'd slept pretty much continuously since late the night before when they had arrived at the safehouse. He'd passed out on the way up the mountain, and even the jostling of his pack carrying him to the cabin didn't wake him. She'd closed the blinds, but the noontime sun was beating its way around the edges, trying to waken him. She got up and put towels over them, hanging them from the curtain rods at the top to block out even more light.

Just as she was finishing the last one, his voice made her jump.

"Probably easier just to let the sun in."

She whirled toward him, heart hammering. "I just was trying to—"

"I know what you were doing," he said, eyes glittering with mischief. "I've been watching you for the last half hour."

Her mouth dropped open.

"Come here." He held out a hand, gesturing her over. It wasn't a command, although he could have used his command voice on her, now that she'd submitted to him. But the truth was, with him sitting up in a rumpled bed with no shirt and his hair mussed in a bed-head kind of way, sleepy-eyed with that lazy, half-awake smile… well, overpowered futuristic militia from her game *AfterPulse* couldn't keep her out of that man's bed.

She quickly crossed the room, and just barely resisted the urge to jump into the bed—she'd been waiting all morning for him to recover enough to wake up. Instead, she eased gently onto the mattress next to him.

"Well, that's nowhere near close enough." He pulled her into his lap.

She let him but tried to be careful about it, gently running her hands over the dozens of scars on his chest. "Are you sure I'm not hurting you?"

He nuzzled into the crook between her shoulder and her neck. "You mean that little dance your hands are doin' on my chest? You keep torturing me like that, and you won't be wearing clothes much longer."

She grinned and tilted her head, offering her neck to him. A growl rumbled in his chest as he nipped and kissed his way up to her jaw. She sucked in a breath, her heart racing with his touch. She'd never wanted something so badly as she wanted Owen Harding to strip off her clothes and claim her.

But he stopped at her jawline and pulled back.

She glared at him. "I've been waiting all morning for

this. Don't tell me you're not healed enough to kiss me."

He bit his lip, but it was doing a poor job of holding back the grin. "Oh, I'm definitely healed enough for that. And a whole lot more, baby girl. But don't you have a company you should be running?" He peered intently into her eyes.

"I have something more important to do." She leaned down to kiss him, and she gave it her complete attention—one hand in his hair, the other splayed across his chest. She could feel the unevenness of his scars under her fingertips, rough over the hard steel of his muscles, but knowing how he got them and why... they just turned her on even more. If that was possible. Wetness was already starting to pool between her legs. She explored his mouth with her tongue, and he let her have free rein, but he couldn't miss the scent of her arousal. He had to know how much she wanted him. She certainly didn't miss the hard flagpole of his cock rising between them and pressing into her. Her hand slipped down his chest, shoved aside the blanket, and grabbed hold of it through his sleep pants.

His answering groan to her stroke just made her body ache more for him.

But he grabbed hold of her wrist and pulled her hand

away. Then he broke their kiss.

"Nova." His voice was hoarse. "Tell me again that you want me. That you want *my bite*. Because I swear to God, now that you've made this submission bond between us... I've spent the last half hour telling myself I can't just wake up and ravage you immediately. That I need to ask you if you're sure—"

She stopped him with fingers to his lips. "I'm sure."

"We can wait—"

"I can't wait." God, she wanted to jump this gorgeous man. "Why do you think I've been sitting here by your bedside for the last twelve hours?"

One side of his mouth tipped up. "Because you wanted to nurse me back to health?"

She gave an exaggerated sigh. "Well, yes, that, too." Then reached down to pull off her t-shirt. She wasn't wearing anything underneath. Satisfaction coursed through her as Owen's gaze immediately dropped to her bare breasts, which, since she was on his lap, were within licking distance of that talented tongue of his—and he damn well better use it on her.

But instead of tasting her, he ran his tongue along his own lips, then slid his hand up to cup her breast. He groaned and looked back into her eyes. "Nova," he warned.

She held his hand to her breast, encouraging him. The rumble in his chest grew louder.

"I've been waiting for you to wake up," she said, her own breathing starting to get short, "because there was no way I was leaving your side and taking the chance of Brad finding me and claiming me. Not when I've already given my heart to you."

His hand stilled on her breast, which just made her pout. "I have your heart?"

"Yes." She leaned into him, practically begging him to give attention to her body, not her eyes, which he was staring deeply into.

"That's only fair," he whispered. "Because you've had mine from the beginning." He pulled her down into a kiss, and this time he was serious. He worked her breast and plundered her mouth, then quickly slid her off his lap and onto the floor. His hands left her, and a small sound of protest escaped her, but then she saw he was working his sleep pants off with record speed. She only got her jeans partly unbuttoned before his hands were shoving hers away and roughly yanking her jeans down.

"Step out of the damn pants, Nova," he growled. She felt the thrill of the command flush through her, and she worked as fast as she could out of them. As soon as she was free, he grabbed hold of her hips and lifted her from the floor, literally tossing her onto the bed. She almost laughed... until he pounced on her with a lust-crazed look that nearly stopped her heart. Her hands went to his chest, looming above her, but he just grabbed them and yanked them over her head, trapping them against the sheets. He held them together with one hand while the other dove between her legs and cupped her sex.

"You're so wet for me," he panted against her neck. Then he thrust two fingers inside her. She arched up, gasping and half-shrieking with the suddenness of it. As he pumped her, ramping her fast and hard toward orgasm, his mouth suddenly clamped onto her aching breast, sucking and nipping and lapping at her, rubbing his face all over her chest as moved from one side to the other. He was *tasting* her, devouring her, holding her still while he ravished her with just his tongue and his fingers.

"Owen!" she cried as the sweet pressure built between her legs. She wanted so much more from him. *All* of him.

He growled, moving his mouth up to feast on her neck while still pumping her toward her released. "You are *mine*. All mine. Forever mine."

"Yes," she gasped. Then the orgasm took her, breaching her walls and breaking her down, one giant, savage wave of pleasure that crashed through her like a wrecking ball. She bucked hard against him, her body succumbing to the wave and to his hands, one still holding her pinned above, the other wrenching pleasure from her below.

Dear God in heaven... how did she get so lucky as to call this man her own?

Suddenly, he released her, but before she could protest, his hands were on her hips again, flipping her over on the bed, then pulling her rear end up into the air. He was positioning to take her from behind, and she barely got her hands under her before he slammed his cock inside.

She gasped and then moaned with the fullness of it. Before she could even begin to adjust, he was pulling back and slamming into her again and again, gripping her hips to hold her against the onslaught. He was wild with her—more wild even that their most fervent lovemaking before, that one night in her bed when they spent half the night coupled one way or another. This was different— he was claiming her hard with his cock, branding her with his need, even before his fangs came out.

This was the moment she had been waiting for—the hot lovemaking she had always been promised was due to mated couples—and her heart surged with happiness that this was happening with a man she loved more than anything. And his savage need for her, the press of his fingers into her hips, his groaning, grunting pleasure as he took her… it was better than her hottest, wildest fantasies had ever been.

"Oh, God, Owen," she called out, ready to cry with all the feelings trapped inside her, building like the orgasm he was rocketing her towards.

"Fuck, you are so good," he breathed, his voice ragged. Then one of his hands left her hip, sliding up her back as he leaned over her. She felt his hand in her hair, fisting and yanking her head back even as he was still pounding into her.

God, she was so close. *Again.* Her entire body clenched with anticipation of the orgasm, then she shuddered as she felt his hot breath on her shoulder, leaning forward to claim her with his bite. The small sounds of pleasure that were escaping her—the moans and gasps and whimpers—were nothing compared to the growling, grunting above her.

She felt him trail his fangs across her back. "Tell me

you're mine," he breathed, voice shaky with need.

"I'm yours." No truer words had ever been spoken. "Take me!"

He roared and sunk his fangs into her. The pain pushed her over the edge, and her body exploded with pleasure. White hot heat poured into her—Owen's magic—from the bite, swirling in and filling her from the inside out with his magic while his cock stretched and filled her as well. Wave after wave of the orgasm wrecked her, making every part of her quiver with pleasure. His groans reverberated through her flesh as his mouth clamped onto her. Then he slammed deep inside her and stilled, the guttural moan echoing the pulsing she could feel as he came. He held her that way, tight and close, piercing her with his cock and his fangs for a moment longer, then he released her completely, falling to the side into the pillows.

Her whole body shivered with the absence of him for a split second until he pulled her down to him as well.

"Holy fuck," he whispered, gathering her up to his chest, cuddling her close. She couldn't get much closer without having him inside her again, but that wasn't what made her feel like their souls had been seared together. *That* was the magic working its way through her system.

Her heart was soaring, her mind wiped clean of anything and everything other than the gorgeous man breathing heavily beside her, still coming down from his own release. She snuggled closer into his arms, placing soft kisses on his neck and face and nuzzling him the way they had when she first pledged her submission to him.

Her heart trembled at how close she had been to making the wrong decision. *The wrong man.* In a way, Owen had been the wrong man for her from the start— not in her pack, not able to take a mate, the forbidden bodyguard—until she realized he was exactly what she needed to break her out of the predetermined fate that Brad and even her father had envisioned for her. A fate that was of their choosing, not hers. Owen had come along and stirred her around and made her realize she could truly make her own choices.

He had saved her in so many ways. And not a moment too soon.

His hands found her face, softly touching her everywhere. "How did I get so lucky?" he whispered.

She pulled back to look at him. "You're not the lucky one here, soldier. That's pretty clearly *me.*"

He grinned, and she loved the look of joy on his face. It actually brought tears to her eyes, which she fought hard to beat back. She didn't want him to think she had anything but happiness raging through her with his magic filling every cell of her body.

"I hope I can always trick you into believing that, Ms. Wilding." His eyelids dropped to half-mast, that hooded look sending fresh shivers through her. "Or convince you by some means." His tongue sneaked out to lick his lips, like he was getting ready to *taste* her again—another thought that sent flushes of heat racing through her.

"What? You mean we're doing this more than *once?*" she asked with a smirk.

His eyes flashed with a bit of that wildness again. *God,* he was killing her with that. Then his arms hardened around her, and before she could blink, he'd flipped her over again, trapping her between his gorgeous, hard-muscled body and the mattress. His eyes feasted on her, drawing a long, hot stare across her skin.

"It's never going to be *Game Over* for me, not with the smoking hot mate I have." The hungry look in his eyes was quickly followed by the growing hardness of his cock between them. It was like the one night they had shared before—the man had amazing recovery time, and he used every inch of it. She was going to be sore tomorrow— deliciously, deliriously sore.

He dipped his head to nip at her neck and before she could even ease into the rhythm of his skin on hers, he was already inside her again. Slow and languorous this time. Hot as a Texas day and twice as sexy, Owen slowly worked her body. He knew just where to touch, just how hard and how soft, and if she hadn't already lost her heart to him, she would have given it over, tied in a bow, right then, just to always have this man in her bed.

"You'll always be mine, Nova Wilding."

She found his eyes and stared deep into them. "Yes."

And the rest of the night was just their bodies speaking an endless echo of those words.

CHAPTER 19

Two days after the kidnapping, Owen was back on the job.

Only now "the job" was a whole lot more complicated. He still considered his job to primarily be keeping Nova Wilding alive, but now he was also expected to help her lead the pack. He had no problem with that—the Army had taught him plenty about leadership, and in spite of Brad's dramatic departure, most of the pack had been more than willing to submit to him when he and Nova returned to the office this morning. He was flush with the magical energy of all those submissions, and he could see Nova's energy level go through the roof as well. It made him want to christen her office with the lovemaking they had been having pretty much non-stop since they mated.

But it was time to return to the real world.

And in that world, the one outside the safehouse cabin where they had celebrated their mating, Owen wasn't at all convinced the danger to her and the other Wilding wolves had passed. Something Nova had said kept nagging at him—that maybe the psycho who had kidnapped her, Tommy Rachet, wasn't actually the Wolf Hunter.

Owen had paced the extent of the Wylderide offices as much as he could stand, and he knew Nova was busy trying to launch her game, but he couldn't help knocking on her office door and interrupting her.

He poked his head in. "Hey, baby girl, you got a minute?"

She didn't look up from her screen. "You keep calling me baby girl in the office, and we're going to have a problem."

He smirked and came in, closing the door behind him.

"The kind of problem that can be solved with my relentless charm and wit?"

She smiled, still not looking up. "The kind that might be forgotten under a barrage of hot kisses."

So... he wasn't the only one who hadn't gotten enough yet. He suspected he never would. He crossed the office in three strides, swerved around the edge of the desk, spun her chair to face him, leaned her chair back and kissed her thoroughly. She was half giggling through the whole thing, and that certainly wouldn't do.

He snapped her chair back up, hauled her out of it, and hoisted her small body up by hips, walking her back toward the cot she kept shoved off to the side. Definitely time to christen the office.

He had her down on the mattress before she could even start to protest.

"Owen, *God!*" she said, trying to shove him away from his growling kisses on her neck.

"It's a little early to start praying my name, baby girl." He chuckled. "You've got to give me a chance to warm you up."

"Oh. My. God." She drew out the words. "We are *not* making love in my office."

"Not yet." He slipped a hand under her t-shirt.

ALISA WOODS

She squirmed deliciously underneath him. "You cannot... we *can't*, Owen..." She was fighting him so desperately hard, it was both turning him on and making laughter bubble up from deep inside him.

"Well, we certainly *can*. This weekend is all the proof I need—" He was cut off by the door flying open.

Nova let out a small shriek, and the guy at the door with the laptop nearly dropped it.

"I... um... I'll just..." The man was gesturing helplessly, like he was frozen by the embarrassment of finding them tangled up on the cot.

Owen rolled his eyes and heaved himself up from the cot. Nova had already wiggled out from underneath him anyway.

"No! It's fine. We were just..." Nova was frantically straightening her clothes. "What do have there, Scott?" She pointed to the laptop.

Scott was still frozen in the half-open doorway, mouth working, like he wasn't sure what to do.

"Come on, man," Owen said with a dramatic sigh. "You've already interrupted us. Make it worth it."

Scott gave him a nod, and the grim set to his mouth wiped the smile off Owen's face. The man brought his laptop around to where Nova and Owen could both see.

A list of emails and other documents filled the screen. It didn't mean anything to Owen, but Nova seemed to immediately know what it was.

"Oh, shit." She held a hand to her mouth in horror.

"Yeah," Scott responded.

"Um?" Owen asked, looking between the two of them.

Scott gestured to the screen. "I've been searching through the computer we recovered, you know, from the... the scene of the crime." He was talking about Nova's kidnapping but obviously didn't want to call it what it was—a torture room.

"You mean Tommy Rachet's computer," Owen said.

Scott let out a sigh. "Yes. And he's definitely the one who doxed the Wilding and River packs. Somehow he'd accessed our servers and pulled out all kinds of stuff. There are raw dumps of data all over his computer, and all kinds of private name and addresses show up."

Owen peered at Nova. "That's good, right? Now we know he's the guy."

"Well, not really." Scott tapped on the laptop and brought up another screen. One with a video. "This was just uploaded today."

The frozen start screen was definitely the Wolf

Hunter.

"Today?" Nova asked, still looking horrified.

Owen scowled at the screen. "Could it have been recorded earlier and just uploaded now?"

Scott shook his head. "It was a live feed earlier today." He started playing the video.

"A lot of you have been leaving comments about the latest shifter video," the Wolf Hunter intoned with his creepy, modulated voice. He had the same mask as the original doxing video, same voice changer. Owen knew Rachet's videos had a similarly styled mask, but he'd never bothered to change his voice. Something Owen had missed before.

Then a two second loop started to play of a large, white wolf slicing Tommy Rachet to pieces.

"Oh, shit," Owen whispered.

"What about the part where I was tortured?" Nova asked, outraged. "Where's that!"

Owen slipped his arm around her. She shouldn't have to watch this again. "Shut it off," he said to Scott.

The man frowned. "There's just that part in the beginning. You should watch the rest."

Owen grimaced, but Nova nodded, so he let it go.

The looping stopped, and the Wolf Hunter in his

mask returned. "Do you see the danger they present? Do you see why they must be stopped? Use any means necessary, my fellow True Humans, but show the shifters that you are not intimidated by them. Lure them in, use their ways against them, but make them pay for the crimes against humanity they've committed." The Wolf Hunter leaned closer to the camera. "The white wolves are a special danger. You saw what this monster is capable of."

Nova's hand found his. The FBI had questioned her and her staff and even Owen, but they couldn't ID the wolf DNA at the scene of the crime. *Owen's blood.* They couldn't prove he was the one who killed Tommy Rachet, even if it was in self-defense.

The video continued with the Wolf Hunter giving another one of his hate-filled screeds. Owen tapped the screen to end it.

"I'm sorry," Scott said. "But I thought you'd want to know right away."

"No, you did good," Owen said.

Nova nodded her approval as well.

"So what are we going to do?" Scott asked.

Owen could feel the flush of magic, the trust that Scott had from submitting to him, that Owen would lead the way in this crisis. But it wasn't just a crisis for Nova. Or even Wylderide.

He squeezed Nova a little tighter. "We launch the game. We live our lives. We don't let this bastard ruin any of that. But, yeah… it's clear that no Wilding is safe until we stop this guy."

Scott gave him a nod and retreated with his laptop.

Owen drew Nova into his arms and kissed the top of her head. "He didn't say anything about you. He's not targeting you specifically. You and your dad… that was all about Tommy Rachet, and he's dead now."

She nodded against his chest, holding him tight. After a moment, she leaned back. "I'm not really worried about myself anymore. I'm worried about every other Wilding out there. And any wolf who falls into this guy's crosshairs."

Owen nodded and drew her back. "I know."

Rachet was dead, but the Wolf Hunter still lived. And how many other Rachets would there be out there, vigilantes who would blame shifters for their inadequate lives and take out their frustrations by hunting down and killing wolves? Owen would do everything he could to protect his new mate and his new pack from the dangers, but there was no doubt…

It was a dangerous time to be a wolf.

Want more Wilding Pack?
WILD LOVE (Wilding Pack Wolves 2)

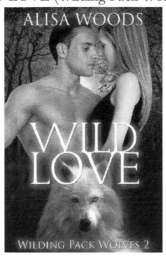

SWIPE RIGHT FOR WILDLOVE!
She programs a dating app for shifters.
He's an ex-Army shifter with a dark secret.
The human and shifter worlds are about to collide…
Get WILD LOVE today!

Subscribe to Alisa's newsletter to know when a new book
is coming out!
http://smarturl.it/AlphaLoversNews

ABOUT THE AUTHOR

Alisa Woods lives in the Midwest with her husband and family, but her heart will always belong to the beaches and mountains where she grew up. She writes sexy paranormal romances about alpha men and the women who love them. She enjoys exploring the struggles we all have, where we resist—and succumb to—our most tempting vices as well as our greatest desires. She firmly believes that love triumphs over all.

All of Alisa's romances feature sexy alphas and the strong women who love them.